P9-APL-259

Lorette Wilmot Library
Nazareth College of Rochester

DEMCO

little chicago

Also by Adam Rapp

Missing the Piano
The Buffalo Tree
The Copper Elephant
Nocturne: A Play

little chicago

adam rapp

FRONT STREET
Asheville, North Carolina

WITHDRAWN

LORETTE WILMOT LIBRARY
NAZARETH COLLEGE

Copyright © 2002 by Adam Rapp

All rights reserved

Printed in the United States

Designed by Helen Robinson

FIRST EDITION

CIP data is available

Library of Congress control number is 2002019269

JF
Rap

little chicago

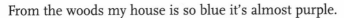

From the woods my house is so blue it's almost purple.

It is after the night and a light has been left on in the kitchen window.

The moon is still in the sky. It looks gray and heavy.

There's the night and there's after the night but the name for this keeps getting lost in my head.

The path is hard to follow but my legs move through the plants and sticks. There are rocks and garbage, too. The trees smell like pepper.

My legs are okay, I tell myself. My legs are good.

The air is cold and I'm shivering so much I wonder if I'll be able to stop. It's like when you get the hiccups.

I see some birds and this helps matters. They are black with small eyes and when they spring from a branch they shriek like people.

It's the morning, I tell myself. It's the morning.

When I come out of the woods I walk through the field and past the dead Ford Taurus. The mud is hard and black and there are shriveled cornstalks everywhere.

The sky looks metallic. The clouds are flat like fish.

My legs are still okay, I tell myself. My feet sting but my legs are okay.

In the back seat I see an empty case of Milwaukee's Best beer and several smashed cans. The early morning light makes the Ford Taurus look like it grew right out of the field. Like a farmer planted a car seed and never came back to harvest it.

Someone has stolen the steering wheel.

What would you do with a steering wheel? What would you use it for?

I touch the antenna. It is chilly and numb-feeling.

And there's my hands, too, I tell myself. My hands are okay, too.

Our backyard is swampy with dew. The grass is brown and colder than I thought it would be. The slime comes up through my toes. But it's a small yard and there's not much farther to go.

I walk under the swing set and past the poplar tree.

There's a cat up in the branches. He's gray with white stripes and he's staring at me like I'm the cat and he's the human.

Hey, I say to it with my mind. I try to use my mouth but it's not working.

I slip through the patio doors and stand in the kitchen.

I am breathing, I tell myself. There is air in me and I am using it.

The kitchen smells like tuna and dirty dishes. On the stove someone has left a glob of Velveeta Shells & Cheese in a pot. I poke at it and it's hard like a rock.

From my reflection in the window I can see that there's a brown leaf stuck to my chest. My hair is wet and matted. When I touch the leaf I can feel my heart squirming like an animal.

My heart's still working, I say. My heart works, too.

My feet sting more now and there's blood so I wrap them in Bounty paper towels with two-ply absorbency.

The refrigerator hums like it's praying. I look inside. There is a package of bologna and other items but my stomach feels sick so I close it.

The clock over the toaster says six-thirty but I know this is not the right time cause it's been stuck this way forever.

I peel the leaf off my chest and put it in the sink like it's a plate.

My fingers are okay, I say. My fingers work, too.

I walk down the hall and knock on my sister's door. I can hear her sleeping on the other side. Her breathing is deep and warm-sounding.

I knock again cause I feel like I'm disappearing. Somehow the knocking keeps this from happening.

My hands are scraped raw from the woods.

When Shay opens the door she leans against it like her bones are too heavy. She is wearing her Moby shirt and

nothing else. The Moby shirt is red with blue letters and it goes down to her knees.

Her toenails are red. The other day I saw her coloring them with a Sharpie permanent marker.

She says, What time is it, Blacky?

Her eyes are half closed and mascara is smeared below her lids. She smells like cigarettes and hairspray.

I open my mouth to talk but no words come out. Instead I sort of baa like a sheep.

Shay wipes snots from her nose and looks at me for a second. Her nostrils are pink and raw.

How come you're naked? she says.

I make a fist in front of my genitals.

She says, Do you realize you're naked, Blacky?

I try to speak again but my throat feels like there's a fist in it. I want to tell her how I found a newspaper in the woods and how I was using it like clothes. I had it wrapped around my waist but it was wet and it kept falling apart.

Shay squints and says, And your feet. What happened to your feet?

I open my mouth and baa again.

I saw a sheep at a petting farm once. It had a face like a president.

Shay takes my head between her hands. Her breath smells like Doritos Cool Ranch tortilla chips and alcohol.

Talk to me, Blacky, she says. Talk to me.

Feeling her hands on my face makes me pant.

I was over at Al's, I finally say between breaths.

My voice sounds small and dead. I have to swallow that fist to talk again.

I just got home, I say. I was over at Al's.

You just got home?

I nod so hard my chin hits my chest.

Shay says, It's five-thirty in the fuckin morning, Blacky.

My neck works, too, I think, nodding more. My neck still works.

Ma let you spend the night on a Sunday?

I say, I had my toothbrush. Al was gonna drive me to school.

Shay looks like she's shrinking right there in her doorway. Like someone's pulling her away with a rope.

I want to go to her bed and climb under the covers. I want her to tuck me in and fluff the pillow.

Blacky, what's wrong with your feet? You're bleeding all over the place.

I feel an ache in my chest like I might cry.

They got cut in the woods when I crossed the creek, I explain. I was staying the night.

Shay crouches down and examines the paper towels.

She says, You got scratches all over your legs. Do you see how many cuts you got? She touches them and says, They're everywhere, Blacky.

There's black polish on her fingernails, too. Either that or they got smashed.

I say, Is Ma home yet?

She don't get home till seven-thirty, Shay says, standing back up. Her hair is red and wavy like Ma's. And her eyes are bluer than the house.

Shay says, Blacky, did somethin happen at Al's?

I was staying the night and then I woke up, I explain. I was staying the night...

Shay takes me by the shoulders and looks me square in the face. Her pupils look like they're shrinking.

She says, Did Al do somethin to you, Blacky?

But I just go blank.

What did that motherfucker do?

Sometimes I wish I was a fish. This way I could breathe when I'm drowning.

I left my clothes there, I say. My Bears jersey and my toothbrush. I couldn't get my Nikes, either.

Shay says, Forget your Nikes!

I need em for Gym, I say. I need em.

This is so fucked, she says. I'm callin Betty and we're takin you to St. Joe's.

Then Shay turns and pulls on a pair of sweatpants and her green flip-flops.

For a second it's like I'm there but I'm missing at the same time. There's a poster on her wall but I can't figure out what's on it. I used to know this information. I even knew it yesterday.

Shay says, Go put some clothes on, Blacky. Go now!

When I try to turn toward my room I have to stop cause I realize that I'm urinating on the floor. It just comes out like water through a spout.

Shay says, Oh no, not in the hall, not in the hall.

Then she hugs me and helps me to the bathroom and my head goes real heavy but I aim so the last bit makes it into the toilet bowl.

Shay is crying and hugging me and saying, It's okay, Blacky. Everything's gonna be okay...

2

When I wake up I'm lying on a padded hospital table with paper on it. The paper is cold and crinkles.

My head hurts.

My mouth is dry and tastes like a spoon.

A nurse in a white uniform is standing over me. She smells like gum and Jergens lotion.

I'm wearing clothes now and the light is harsh.

Somewhere I can hear Shay's and Betty's voices like bees buzzing on a window.

Hello, Blacky, the nurse says. She is tall with brown hair and she has a face like a hawk's.

Where am I? I say.

The nurse says, You're on the second floor of St. Joseph's Hospital. Your sister and her friend brought you in a little while ago.

Her voice is gentle and strong at the same time.

Shay must have got the clothes on me, I think. Shay did it.

I am wearing a pair of jeans from T.J. Maxx, a white T-shirt from my laundry pile, and my black Sunday shoes. The shirt smells damp and moldy. My shoes feel tight in the toes.

Would you like something to drink? the nurse asks.

I nod and she gives me a 7-Up with a straw. Like she saw it in her head and then it just appeared in her hand that way.

There's a black blood-pressure thing wrapped around my arm. While I drink from the straw the nurse puffs it up and makes it leak. My muscle swells so thick I think it might burst.

Is Shay still here? I ask.

The nurse says, She's next door speaking to Dr. Darius. We're just going to get some of these cuts cleaned up and then the doctor will need to examine you.

My ma works here, I say. She's a radiology technician. She's up on the fourth floor.

But the nurse doesn't register this fact. She's too busy removing the blood-pressure thing from my arm.

Can you take your shoes off for me? she asks.

Okay, I say, but my hands won't move. I stare at them for a second like they're someone else's hands.

Do you want me to help you, Blacky?

I can do it, I say, and then my hands finally move and I take off my Sunday shoes. The nurse sets them on the floor and opens a brown bottle.

What's that? I ask.

It's iodine, she says. It kills germs. We don't want any of those cuts on your feet to get infected.

Her breath is warm and minty-smelling.

This might sting a bit, she says, pouring the stuff over a cotton ball. It's orange and smells like it will hurt.

Just relax, she says. Breathe easy ...

While she cleans my feet I jerk and flinch.

There, there, now, the nurse says. There, there ...

Then she dabs at the scrapes on my arm and the backs of my hands. After she bandages my feet I just sit there and drink the 7-Up. It's so cold it hurts my teeth but I finish the whole can in about a minute.

When I look up the nurse is gone and a tall African American man with a mustache is standing there. I didn't even hear the door. It's like he was hiding under the table.

Hello, Blacky, he says. I'm Dr. Darius. His voice is deep like a song.

Hello, I say.

He takes a step closer and takes my hand and looks at the cuts. He says, I bet that smarts, huh?

I nod and then he undoes his jacket and checks his watch. His mustache looks like he bought it at a store.

He says, I understand that you've had quite a morning. How are you feeling?

Okay, I say.

Your sister filled me in on some of the details.

His uniform is so white it almost hurts to look at. I try to drink from the 7-Up again but it's empty and I wind up making slurping noises.

Would you like another one? the nurse suddenly asks.

I have no idea how she got back in the room. I didn't even see the door open.

When I was running through the creek I thought I heard Al Johnson whispering my name. It made me run faster and I slipped and fell in the rocks.

... Blacky? the nurse says.

My hands are okay, I think. My hands are still attached to my wrists and they're working just fine.

Would you like another can of pop? Dr. Darius says.

Yes, please, I say.

Then the nurse leaves and when she opens the door I can see into the hall. Shay and Betty are talking to a woman with frizzy hair. The woman is writing things down on a yellow pad. Shay's doing most of the talking. Betty's just sort of standing there. She's wearing a blue bathrobe and her face looks dead.

When the door closes, Dr. Darius says, Blacky, this might be a little uncomfortable, but I'm going to have to examine you for a moment.

I'm okay, I say.

I know you might feel that way, Dr. Darius says. But we have to make sure.

Then the nurse comes back in the room with my 7-Up and another straw, but she doesn't give it to me this time.

She just stands there like the police.

I say, What do you need to examine?

Dr. Darius says, Your rectum.

What's a rectum? I ask.

Your bottom, he says. The part you use when you go to the bathroom.

Why? I say.

Because we have to be sure about certain things.

I'm sure, I say.

I know you're sure, Blacky. But *we* have to be sure, too. It's part of the procedure. Would that be okay?

My ma works on the fourth floor, I say. She's a radiology technician.

We know that, Blacky. In fact at this very moment she's right next door to this room speaking to a woman from Children's Services. The sooner we get this done, the sooner you can see your mother, okay?

My ma's right next door? I ask.

Dr. Darius says, In the room just to our left, yes.

The nurse nods and makes a kind face.

Dr. Darius says, So if you'll take your pants down for me we'll get this over with real quick. There's nothing to worry about. I promise it won't hurt.

I nod and look down at my feet. The medicine is soaking through the bandages. It looks like spilled orange juice.

While I'm undoing my pants Dr. Darius puts white rubber gloves on. They make his hands look huge and fake.

I lower my underwear. I can see that these were taken out of the laundry pile, too. In fact, I notice from the size that they're actually my little brother's. Cheedle's a small and I'm a medium.

The room is cold and I feel myself shrinking.

Dr. Darius says, I'll need you to bend over for me so I can examine your rectum, okay?

The nurse won't look at my penis. She's looking at the 7-Up instead. She's looking at it so hard I think she might drink it.

Dr. Darius says, Bend down and touch your toes. Can you do that for me, Blacky?

Yes, I say.

We do toe touches in Gym. Toe touches and burpies. Coach Corcoran calls out eight counts. He always slows down at around six.

I reach down and touch my toes. Dr. Darius opens my butt. His hands are huge and warm.

Just relax, Blacky, he says. This will be over before you know it.

I feel like I have to urinate. A drop even falls on the floor.

Sorry, I say to the nurse.

But she just keeps looking at the 7-Up in her hand.

How old are you, Blacky? Dr. Darius asks from behind me.

Eleven, I say. I'm eleven but I'll be twelve soon.

When's your birthday?

November seventeenth, I say.

Sixth grade? he asks.

Yes, I say.

He's using something metal to open me up more now. It's cold on my butt. I imagine one of those tools you use in a garden.

He's gardening, I tell myself. It's okay cause he's just gardening...

What's your favorite subject in school? Dr. Darius asks.

I don't know, I say. Not dodgeball.

He laughs. His laugh is on my back like a cat.

Very good then, he says. You can pull your pants up.

I pull up my jeans and stand there for a moment. I don't turn around cause I feel stuck. Shay didn't use a belt and I have to keep my hands in my pockets so they won't fall back down.

I realize that there is no window in this room and it makes me feel trapped.

Are you okay, Blacky? the nurse asks.

I nod even though I'm still facing the other way.

I can feel Dr. Darius trying to communicate with the nurse behind my back. They're talking the way aliens talk. It's all about brainwaves and the eyes.

When I turn around he is gone.

Doctors are magicians in white coats and I think I'm forgetting how time works.

The nurse is still standing there with my 7-Up.

You can put your shoes back on, she says.

I watch my hands for a moment and then I put on my Sunday shoes.

Is Shay out there? I ask.

She left with her friend a few minutes ago, the nurse says.

I say, What about my ma?

She says, I'm not sure, Blacky. But Ms. Wolf from Children's Services would like to speak with you now. So if you'll follow me.

When we go into the hall, Ma is slumped in a chair and she is talking to two policemen.

Ma, I say. Ma.

She looks up at me.

Hi, honey, she says.

Her face is wet and puffy. She is holding several crumpled tissues. The hospital light makes her hair seem redder than it does at home.

She reaches out and squeezes my hand. It makes the scrapes sting but I don't care.

The policemen are huge and their faces look like concrete.

All the people in the hall seem sad and near death with boredom. There's a woman sitting on the floor and she's eating a McDonald's cheeseburger. She is so fat it looks like her body hurts.

And there's this nun walking around with no eyebrows. She's all in black and you can't see her feet. It's like she's floating around vampire style.

Where'd Shay go? I ask.

Ma says, She reeked of alcohol so I told her to go away. She left with Betty.

She blows her nose and starts scratching her arms. She's got this thing called eczema. She uses creams that smell like vegetable soup and metal. Once I walked into the kitchen and her neck was so red it could have been hamburger meat. She was leaning against the refrigerator and clawing away.

Sometimes I imagine her with no skin, just all her veins and various tissues.

Ma's got a depression problem, too. She took medication for a while but she stopped cause she said the pills made her feel loopy.

I think she gets depressed cause she works around all these sad people. Maybe sadness is like chicken pox and other contagious diseases.

Ma, I wanna go home, I say.

My throat gets that ache in it again.

She squeezes my hand again and says, In a few minutes, Blacky. After you talk to Ms. Wolf, okay?

Okay, I say, but I feel stuck.

Ma says, Go talk to Ms. Wolf. She's a nice lady.

One of the policemen says, Follow the nurse now, son.

His face looks less like concrete when he talks but I still have this feeling that he'll arrest me if I don't obey his orders.

I look over my shoulder to see if Dr. Darius is back but he's not.

Then I turn and follow the nurse into the other room.

The woman standing behind the desk smells like ham.

I recognized this odor when I walked in the room. Ham smells guilty and I imagine her doing stuff. Stuff like shoplifting or spitting in a pan.

She's the one with the frizzy hair who was talking to Shay and Betty in the hall. She wears a long-sleeved yellow shirt with a collar and brown pants. Her clothes seem too big for her body.

It's like she's trying to hide in them.

The badge on her shirt says:

WENDY WOLF

CHILDREN'S SERVICES

It sounds like a name you would make up. Like Bob Bear or Sam Snake.

There's a desk and a window and a chair that is the color of lima beans. Other than this there are very few items in the room.

Hello, Gerald, she says, holding out her hand. I'm Ms. Wolf.

Hello, I say, and take another step into the room.

I shake her hand. Her fingers feel long and warm.

I'm glad to meet you, she says. Please take a seat.

I sit in the chair. My feet are starting to itch from all that orange stuff.

On the wall behind the Ham Lady there's a United Way poster of a kid with bruises. He's staring at me like he's hungry.

Are you comfortable? the Ham Lady asks. Is there anything I can get you?

No, thank you, I say.

I realize that I'm holding the 7-Up. It's cold and heavy in my hand. I don't even remember when the nurse gave it to me.

It must have been in the hall, I think. She gave it to me in the hall ...

Outside I can hear my ma pleading with the policeman. Her voice sounds like a clarinet.

There's a clock on the wall. It's bigger than most clocks and I keep thinking it's staring at me like it has a brain. It says it's 8:25.

I'm supposed to be in school, I tell the Ham Lady.

I know, Gerald, she says.

I say, In Math Skills we're doing fractions and prime numbers. I'm gonna miss the bus.

The Ham Lady says, You don't need to worry about that right now.

I say, In Social Studies we're learning about capital punishment. The electric chair and stuff.

She says, You'll be free to go back to school tomorrow, okay?

Okay, I say.

She has this blue ball that she keeps fiddling with. She mostly just rolls it around on her desk but sometimes she squeezes it too.

The Ham Lady looks at me for a second and says, Your mother and I used to work together at Children's Services, did you know that?

No, I say.

It was before she came over here to St. Joe's. I remember when you were born. You and your sister, both...

Once Ma told me she stopped working at Children's Services cause too many kids died.

They just kept dyin, Blacky, she told me. The more they died the more I cried.

While she still worked there, one night she brought home a baby that nobody else wanted. He was African American and his name was Tayshawn Van and he had to crawl around with an air tank strapped to his leg cause of a severe breathing disorder. Sometimes he chirped like a squirrel. He lived with us for a week and then Ma took him somewhere else.

That's when Ma was strong. That was before she got

depressed and had to start taking prescription medication.

I need to ask you some questions, the Ham Lady says. And it might be difficult for you to answer some of them but I want you to do your best to tell the truth, okay, Gerald?

Okay, I say.

She flips a page on her yellow notepad and says, I'd like you to start out by telling me what happened last night when you were with Mr. Johnson.

I don't say anything. Instead I watch the clock. The second hand goes from 3 to 6.

There's no rush, the Ham Lady says. You can take as much time as you need.

I try and take some time but all I can think about is how after I got through the creek I hid behind a tree for several minutes cause I thought I heard Al Johnson whispering again. There was a knot in the bark that looked like a face.

Blacky, I thought I heard Al Johnson say. You forgot your gym shoes, Blacky...

I was sleeping and then I woke up, I tell the Ham Lady. I was in his room.

What were you doing before that?

I say, We were drawing Indians with charcoal pencils. I fell asleep at the kitchen table.

The Ham Lady writes this down and says, Did you and Mr. Johnson draw together a lot?

Yes, I say. We drew stuff and we did copper etchings. He was gonna teach me wood burning, too.

Did you ever draw anything besides Indians?

I say, We drew cows, too. Cows and planes and pictures of presidents. I did one of Calvin Coolidge.

Had you spent the night at Mr. Johnson's before?

Yes, I say.

How many times?

A bunch, I say.

Do you know exactly how many?

No, I say. Maybe like six.

The Ham Lady flips a page and says, Was this the first time he took you into his room like that?

Yes, I say.

In the past when you spent the night where did you sleep?

I say, On the sofa in the living room. It pulls out into a bed.

Did he ever come and visit you while you were sleeping on the sofa?

I say, He gave me some wine once, but that wasn't on the sofa.

Oh, she says. Where was that?

I say, That was in his camper when we were at Seiko State Park.

The Ham Lady writes this information down on her yellow pad. Her voice has hardly changed. It's like they brought her in from the phone company.

Gerald, she says after she's finished writing, did anything ever happen in the camper home?

My name's Blacky, I say.

Oh dear, she says. I'm sorry, Blacky.

Even though her voice is dead she's got a sensitive face. For a second her mouth twitches so much I think it's going to fall off.

Then she says my name again and smiles.

Blacky.

She announces it like she won something.

I listen for Ma in the hall again. I imagine the policemen sitting on both sides of her. They're bored and fiddling with their walkie-talkies.

The Ham Lady says, Isn't Gerald your birth name?

Yes, I say.

Why don't you use it?

I say, Gerald's my dad's name.

I see, she says.

We stopped using it when I was little, I explain.

After he left? she asks.

I don't know, I say. I guess.

She rocks back in her chair and clasps her hands behind her head. Her underarms are sweating and I wonder if they smell more like ham or less like ham.

She says, Who's we?

I say, Who's we what?

You just said we stopped using it when I was little.

Oh, I say. We. Ma and Shay and Cheedle and me.

Shay's your sister and Cheedle's your brother, right?

Yes.

Is Cheedle his real name?

It's Linden but nobody calls him that.

The Ham Lady adjusts her glasses and says, Does Mr. Johnson call you Blacky, too?

Yes, I say.

Does he call you Gerald?

No.

Does he ever call you anything else besides Blacky?

I say, Sometimes.

What else does he call you?

I take a minute.

My hands are still connected to my arms. I make sure to check this, for some reason.

After I came out from behind that tree with the face in it I didn't hear Al Johnson's voice anymore. But I was cold from falling in the creek.

... Blacky? the Ham Lady says.

He calls me Girl, I say.

Girl? she says.

Yes, Girl, I say.

Like the name of a particular girl? she asks.

No, I say. Just Girl.

And how often does Mr. Johnson call you this?

I don't answer.

Does he use this name a lot? she asks.

I say, Sometimes.

Did you call him anything? I mean besides Al or Mr. Johnson.

I never call him Mr. Johnson, I say.

She writes this down. I wait for her to catch up.

Then I add, He has a different name, too.

Oh, she says. What is it?

I think it's possible for your head to pop off at the neck. I can almost feel mine hitting the ceiling.

Blacky, what's Mr. Johnson's different name? she asks.

The lights are buzzing over us. Insects have been trapped and are getting roasted alive. There are certain ways light controls people too, I'm convinced of this.

... Blacky? she says again.

I call him Boy, I say.

For a second she looks like she won't say anything else. Like her voice is a toy that you have to wind up.

I say, When I'm Girl he's Boy.

She makes some more notes on the yellow pad. Every time she writes something new it makes my feet itch.

For some reason I start to think about how when that African American baby lived with us I used to feed him liquid carrots and let him clutch my thumb. His fingers were strong and wrinkled. Once I removed his air mask to feed him and he opened his mouth like he wanted to scream. This was one of the scariest things I've ever seen. I loved him and Ma loved him and Cheedle loved him too, but Shay would call him It and treated him like a science project. Shay sometimes calls African Americans niggers and I'm sure this has something to do with her negative feelings about Tayshawn Van.

After a while the Ham Lady says, So, Blacky, did anything happen when you were with Mr. Johnson in his camper home? When you were down at Seiko State Park?

I say, He just gave me some purple wine to help me sleep.

And you drank it?

Only a little, I say. Ma's had enough problems with Shay's drinking.

The Ham Lady writes some of this down and says, Blacky, can you describe Mr. Johnson's room for me? The room at his house?

I close my eyes to look.

Al Johnson's face is huge in my brain. It's so big it almost stinks.

I drew Calvin Coolidge and he drew General George Washington.

Very good, Blacky, Al Johnson said. Excellent eyes. Excellent, excellent eyes ...

... Blacky? the Ham Lady says.

There were two beds, I say. Two beds on opposite sides.

Were they big beds or little beds?

Little beds, I say. Like bunk beds without the bunks.

She writes again.

I picture her drawing me in one of the beds. My face looks dead and blue.

Anything else? she asks. About the room? Anything at all.

His musket, I say.

She looks up.

She says, His musket?

Yes, I say. He's got a Civil War musket. It's a collector's item. He keeps it in a glass case in front of his bed. It's got this thing called a crosshairs that you look through. He told me he was gonna give it to me someday.

I have to stop talking cause I feel like I'm choking.

I almost have to give myself the Heimlich maneuver to make myself breathe again. We learned about this procedure in Health. There's a colorful poster with the international choking symbol and various first-aid instructions.

The Ham Lady's face goes real still. She says, You okay, Blacky?

I nod.

You sure?

I nod again.

Would you like another 7-Up?

No, thank you, I say.

Talking makes me breathe. It's weird how your body can just stop working at the drop of a dime. Your lungs and stuff.

The Ham Lady is writing again.

I imagine that she's drawing the musket now, too. Maybe she's putting it in the bed with me.

So, Blacky, she says, I know that this is very difficult for you, but I really need you to tell me what happened last night. The exact details of what Mr. Johnson actually did to you.

I find the clock on the wall again. It's ticking so loud I can practically feel it in my teeth.

It's suddenly hailing in the window. You can hear it attacking the hospital.

I think there must be a reason for this.

The Ham Lady doesn't register the hail.

Even though she's sitting across the desk it feels like she's so close that she can look into my mouth and see my tonsils.

Blacky, she says, I know you might feel strange talking about this with your mother in the hall, but I want you to know that you can tell me. I want to help you, okay?

Okay, I say.

We want to make sure that whatever happened to you doesn't happen to anybody else.

What are you gonna do to him? I ask.

I picture Al Johnson sitting where I'm sitting. His face is bald and calm. Then some guy wearing a black mask comes in and chops his head off. A Ninja with a sword.

The Ham Lady says, We're not going to do anything to Mr. Johnson, Blacky. That's not for us to decide. The police and the courts will take care of that, okay?

Okay, I say.

The hail is still coming down. Some of it is hitting the window now. It's so white it looks fake.

So let's get back to what happened, okay, Blacky?

I nod.

So you woke up, the Ham Lady says, and then what?

I woke up and his finger was in me.

Oh, she says. In you where, exactly?

In my butt, I say.

It sounds strange coming out.

Butt.

Like swallowing a bee and barfing.

What finger? the Ham Lady asks. Can you show me what finger?

I show her my thumb.

It's like I'm holding a weapon.

She stares at it like it's going to get her and then she writes on her pad. Maybe she's drawing that, too? Maybe she's drawing Al Johnson's thumb up my butt?

My brain feels warm and small.

The Ham Lady takes her glasses off and cleans them with a tissue. When they're off her eyes look huge and brown.

Did it hurt, Blacky? she asks.

Sort of, I say.

It felt like pooping but I don't tell her this.

Did Mr. Johnson try and put anything else inside of you?

No, I say.

Are you sure? she asks.

Yes, I say. That's when I was running.

I see, she says. And did he run after you?

No, I say.

Did anyone else see you leaving?

His mother.

Where was she?

She was downstairs.

What was she doing?

She was at the table drinking orange water. When I ran by her she called me a heathen. Her name is Merle.

I want to add that she hardly ever spoke to me and that she smelled like a dog and that she's so old she looks painted, but I can't cause my mouth feels funny.

The Ham Lady says, Does Merle live with Mr. Johnson?

Yes, I say. She stays in the bedroom on the first floor. Next to the room with all the bird paintings.

She writes this down, too.

And when you got outside what did you do? the Ham Lady asks.

I ran.

Where did you run to, Blacky?

To the woods.

How far were the woods from his house?

Not far, I say. Just through his backyard.

And you ran all the way home through the woods?

Yes, I say. I walked a little too. And I hid behind a tree when I got tired.

It suddenly occurs to me that when I was hiding behind that tree with the face in it I saw a deer, but I don't tell the Ham Lady this either. The deer froze in some plants. It looked like it was made out of metal. It also looked like it might start singing.

There were lots of mosquitoes, I tell the Ham Lady.

Did you have any clothes on?

No, I say. I found a newspaper but it was wet and it kept falling apart.

How are those cuts on your feet doing? she asks. Do they still hurt?

A little, I say.

Then the Ham Lady takes a drink from her coffee cup and looks inside of it for a moment like there's something in there.

Did Mr. Johnson do anything else, Blacky? she asks. Anything besides touch you with his thumb?

I say, He kissed me.

She writes this down.

I add, He was teaching me how to kiss.

She writes this, too.

After she finishes she stares out the window and says, Oh my God, it's hailing.

The Ham Lady watches it for a moment. I can feel her wanting to go to the window.

If she does this I will leave. I will get Ma and go.

But she doesn't get up.

For some reason I keep thinking about that deer. How its eyes were big and brown. They were the only parts that didn't look metal.

Why are you standing, Blacky? the Ham Lady suddenly asks.

I didn't even realize that this happened. My legs just stood on their own.

Are you okay, honey?

Yes, I say, I'm okay.

Do you need to use the restroom?

No, I say. I didn't... I just...

The Ham Lady says, You just what, Blacky?

But I don't finish. I just stand there and stare at the hail in the window.

You have to wonder about the environment. All that stuff with the greenhouse.

You can sit back down if you'd like, the Ham Lady says.

But I don't sit. I feel better standing.

I say, You're not going to give him capital punishment, are you?

No, Blacky, she says. Mr. Johnson won't get capital punishment, I can promise you that.

We recently learned about this subject in Social Studies. How the electric chair works. All the volts and stuff. I imagine Al's eyeballs exploding on her desk. She'd have to do a thorough job of cleaning cause there's lots of grossness inside us. All types of different snots and liquids.

We're sixty percent water.

Mr. Prisby wrote that on the board in Life Science. Sixty percent, he said, putting the chalk down.

I spent the rest of the day looking at my hand and wondering where all the water was.

In my mind I can hear the electric chair panting like an animal.

I imagine black holes where his eyes were.

Blacky, the Ham Lady says, I want to ask you one more question. It has to do with your mother.

I say, Okay.

I understand that they had gone on a few dates. Did Mr. Johnson ever say anything about her?

Like what?

Anything. Anything at all.

I say, Once he told me that he was gonna marry her so he could be my father.

Would you have liked that, Blacky?

Yes, I say.

Do you think your mother would have liked that?

Yes, I say again.

And your brother and sister?

Shay didn't like him but Cheedle did cause he would listen to his stories.

Did you ever see your mother and Mr. Johnson expressing affection for each other?

What's that? I say.

Affection, Blacky. Emotions. Did you ever see them kiss?

He kissed her on the cheek once, I say. They just got back from Burger King. They were in the kitchen.

She writes this down and then she starts squeezing the blue ball again.

Is there anything else you'd like to tell me? she says. You can tell me anything you'd like, Blacky.

I say, His mouth tasted like a car.

She writes this, too.

For some reason I imagine the Ham Lady naked. All the parts of her body. Her armpits are hairy and her face is all made up like a circus clown's.

I nearly get a boner. It makes me want to run through the window.

Hail in October, the Ham Lady says. Strange.

She watches the hail for a second and then it suddenly stops like she was controlling it.

The hospital feels like it's breathing.

I picture myself hooked up to a bunch of machines with tubes and dials.

The Ham Lady says, Please sit, Blacky.

I don't sit, though. I feel better standing. I'm like a cow.

You sure you don't want another 7-Up? she asks.

I'm sure, I say, staring at the clock. It's 9:07 now.

The minutes feel like forever.

That clock knows more than most people, I think.

Don't hurt him, I say.

For some reason it's like I'm saying it to the clock.

The Ham Lady says, No one's going to hurt Mr. Johnson, Blacky.

I say, If you hurt him I won't say nothin else.

I promise you he's safe, Blacky. The authorities have him now and he's safe.

Then the door opens and one of the policemen makes a private gesture at the Ham Lady.

She nods and says, You can go now, Blacky. Thanks for cooperating. Your mother's waiting for you in the hall.

Come on, son, the policeman says, reaching his hand toward me. I can see the hair on the tops of his knuckles.

I feel stuck again.

Ma's standing in the doorway too now. She's still holding on to the crumpled tissues. There are red streaks all over her arms.

Come on, honey, she says, let's go home.

Your legs are okay, I say to myself. Your legs are good.

When we get home Cheedle's in the living room watching a kung fu movie and writing his novel about a boy raised by a Wisconsin grizzly.

The boy's name is Glen and he is originally from Stevens Point, Wisconsin, and his parents lost him on a fishing trip while they were eating hamburgers and macaroni salad.

Ma got the typewriter at a garage sale on Larkin Avenue for ten bucks. Cheedle puts it on the coffee table and types sitting Indian style. He spends so much time with it I wonder about his relationship to machines. He got that way with Tayshawn Van's air tank. He knew how to refill it and everything.

He types so fast it sounds like a war.

Hey, I say.

He says, Hey.

Ma walks to the back of the house and closes her bedroom

door. In the car she kept trying not to cry but there was a dog on Black Road that got hit and when she saw it she couldn't hold back. The dog was orange and it looked like it was smiling.

What's wrong with her? Cheedle asks, talking while he types.

Nothin, I say.

He says, Unusual entrances always make for good theater.

It's weird when your nine-year-old brother has superpowers. One day Ma took him to Chicago to get tested and later that night this woman named Dr. Evelyn Bush from Northwestern Hospital called and told Ma that Cheedle is a certified genius.

He's a certified genius! Ma announced after she hung up the phone. Your little brother's a genius!

Now Cheedle goes to the Joliet Children's School on Theodore Street. This particular school is for the unusually gifted.

On the TV a man with a cat face is screaming. He punches another man several hundred times. It makes me think that your body can be trained to be invincible. But first you need muscles to start that kind of process.

I wonder when I will get mine.

Did you see the hail? Cheedle asks.

I saw it, I say.

Unusual for October, he says. Some got into our room. I scooped it into a plastic bag and put it in the freezer. It's good to keep samples of such things.

Cheedle has black hair like me. Ma says Cheedle and I got the Black Irish but Shay just got the Irish.

Why didn't you go to school today? he asks.

There was a fire, I say.

I usually don't lie but under the circumstances I feel this is necessary.

The last lie I told happened several months ago. I was talking to a Foot Locker salesman about my shoe size. Once I started I couldn't stop.

What size you got? he asked.

Nine, I said.

That's an awfully big foot for a kid like you.

I have a disease, I told him.

I'm sorry to hear that.

I take medicine to control my growth juices.

Huh, he said.

It went on and on. Twelve lies in a row.

I think this happened cause I couldn't afford the shoes anyway.

It felt like sledding down a hill and letting go of the sides.

Cheedle keeps typing and says, It's good that things burn. The ash enriches the soil.

Whenever I ask him about the novel he says the same thing.

How's the novel coming? I'll ask.

It's coming just fine, he'll say. My hero is in the throes of a dramatic crisis to which there is no foreseeable resolution.

I imagine being raised by a Wisconsin grizzly. It would be hard cause of claws and other bear parts. I hope he is taking all of this into consideration.

Cheedle says, The other day Robert Blyleven saw the Smudge Man.

Really? I say.

The Smudge Man is this half monster that lives in a sewage hole in Hamil Woods. They say he is caked with mud and that he plays the violin. They say his violin music hypnotizes you and that he uses it to lure you down to his hole so he can eat your brain.

Hamil Woods is on the other side of that creek that I fell in. They say that there are deadly water moccasins in this creek but I didn't see any. The creek joins Hamil Woods with the woods behind our house. Unlike Hamil Woods, the woods behind our house doesn't have a name. There's the corn field with the dead Ford Taurus and several scattered pop cans and bicycle parts. A few months ago there was a kitchen sink out there. I walked over and looked at it and there was a sponge stuck to its side. Three days later it was gone. In the summer the field is full of garter snakes and other hard-to-see animals. Once you cross the field there's nothing but trees.

The Ford Taurus just sits out there like it's waiting for something. It's brown with a rusted door.

Where'd he see him? I ask.

Cheedle says, By the softball diamond. His sister had a soccer game and he had to go back to the bleachers to get his backpack. He said that the Smudge Man had his violin and everything.

Did he play it? I ask.

According to Robert Blyleven, no.

Lucky, I say.

Cheedle says, In Art Therapy it became a heated discussion and Jan had us draw our own version of the Smudge Man. I drew him wearing a three-piece herringbone suit and wingtip shoes because I like to think of him as a former trial lawyer. The fallen man. A great literary archetype.

Who's Jan? I ask.

She's our new teacher. She insists that we call her by her first name so as to promote a feeling of egalitarian impartiality.

I have no idea what he's talking about but that's the way it is with Cheedle. There are certain words he'll sometimes use that make me feel like I should never talk again.

On the TV the guy with the cat face jumps several feet in the air and does a flip. When he lands he kicks a giant kung fu beast in the stomach. The giant kung fu beast has silver teeth and he tumbles over a cliff and lands in the sea.

On the other side of Hamil Woods, by Al Johnson's house, there's a bunch of power lines that hum. If you listen to them long enough it's like they're praying. For some reason I can't get the sound of those power lines out of my head.

Is Shay home? I ask.

Not yet, Cheedle says.

It's funny how he has to wear glasses. They're huge and shaped like TV screens. I think he strains his eyes from too much reading. He keeps a book near his bed called *Anna Karenina*. It's so thick it makes me tired just looking at it.

Later I knock on Ma's door.

Come in, she says.

She's lying in bed with her clothes on. It's like she's camping without the tent.

Hey, I say.

Hey, Blacky, she says.

Are you sleeping? I ask.

Just resting.

Are you cold?

No, she replies. Why?

You're wearing your shoes, I say.

She says, I'll take em off later.

Her room is dark and there are books all over the floor. I think Cheedle got the bookworm thing from Ma. She usually stacks the ones she's read against the wall next to her bed, but now they're all scattered like there was an earthquake.

Her green technician's uniform is hanging over the knob on her closet. Once I snuck into her room and put it on. When I looked in the mirror I made a muscle.

Are we gonna eat? I ask.

She says, I'll make some eggs later.

Okay, I say. I could go get some other stuff, too.

She says, That's okay, Blacky. Thanks for offering.

I think about walking to the White Hen Pantry and stealing a Little Tonio microwave burrito. Shay has done this many times. When Ma sends us out to get milk Shay always comes back with one in her pocket. Sometimes she'll eat them cold.

Ma says, Would you get me my creams, Blacky?

I go to her dresser and get her eczema creams. There's change and makeup everywhere. Once I put mascara on my eyebrows. It made me look mean and Hispanic.

In the mirror I can see her in bed. She's still trying to not cry.

I go to the bed and hand her the creams.

Your neck is bleeding, I say.

I know, she says.

Maybe you should put a Band-Aid on it.

I'm okay, she says. It's just on the surface.

She opens her creams and starts to rub them into her neck. It mixes with the blood and makes everything pink and tender-looking.

When she is finished she screws the tops back on the tubes and places them on her stomach.

Then she finally turns to me.

Her eyes are puffy and red. They look like they'd be hot if you touched them.

Ma says, So did you and Wendy have a good talk today?

I say, Who's Wendy?

The woman from Children's Services. Ms. Wolf.

It was okay, I say.

She's a nice person, Ma says. When I worked at Children's Services she always invited me out to lunch.

Then we don't say anything for a minute. You can hear cars going by outside. It sounds like the ocean at the movies.

Ma blows her nose into a tissue and says, It's been a long day, huh?

There is a saliva bubble trapped on her lips.

Yes, I say, and pop the bubble with my finger.

Ma wipes her mouth with the tissue. Then she scratches her neck and the blood starts again.

She says, We'll be okay, okay?

I nod.

I have a double tomorrow. I need to rest, she says, and starts rubbing her eyes.

Some of the blood gets smeared and it makes one of her lids go pink.

She says, I'll come out in a little while and make some eggs, okay?

Okay, I say.

Give me a kiss.

I kiss her on her cheek. It tastes like salt and rubber.

Ma says, See you later, okay?

Okay, I say.

I close the door and go out to the kitchen.

Cheedle is cooking Dinty Moore beef stew in a pot. Only one of the burners functions properly. The oven doesn't work either but a few weeks ago Mom did something ingenious. She brought Shay's old Betty Crocker Easy-Bake Oven up from the basement and now we use that. Cheedle can make just about anything in it. Once he made lasagna and scalloped potatoes.

We'd use the General Electric microwave with turntable cooking, but I accidentally poisoned it by leaving a spoon in a Cup-o-Noodles. Now it just sits on the counter like a pet.

Cheedle says, Want some stew?

No, thanks, I say.

It smells thick and spicy.

He stirs the stew with a wooden spoon. I'm being weak, he says.

I say, Weak how?

According to Anna Beth Coles, Ernest Hemingway said you should always write when you're hungry.

Who's Ernest Hemingway? I ask.

A great American novelist slash boxer slash hunter, he says. He lived in Paris during the Depression and wrote about the Spanish Civil War and bullfighting.

I imagine fighting a bull. It comes at me a hundred miles an hour but I jump out of the way just in time. The crowd throws money at me and a band plays loud music.

Cheedle says, Hunger is a state of mind.

He kills the flame and scoops the stew onto a plate.

Meat and carrots and potatoes.

I suddenly realize that I'm so hungry it feels like there's wind blowing in my stomach.

Cheedle sits at the kitchen table and starts eating.

I use a clean pan to fry two pieces of bologna. Al Johnson used to do this. He also used to take me to Hardee's and Jack in the Box.

But the fried bologna was his specialty.

After I eat the fried bologna I take an egg and crack it into a glass and drink it raw. It tastes like warm snots and I can feel it ooze into my stomach.

I saw this movie called *Rocky* and that's what that guy did. It's good for vitamins and nutrients.

Later, Ma comes out of her room and cooks me some scrambled eggs with Velveeta cheese. She is sleepy and her hair is matted and oily.

Cheedle is in our room making his brain bigger with books and puzzles.

I don't tell Ma I already ate the raw egg and fried bologna. I just pretend I'm still starving.

The heat from the burner makes her eczema act up and she scratches while she cooks. Sometimes Shay catches her using the spatula and lets her know. That's fuckin gross, Ma, she'll say.

Ma burns the scrambled eggs a little but she mixes in just

the right amount of cheese.

We sit together while I eat.

The kitchen light buzzes like it's got a brain.

After a minute I say, I left my Nikes at Al's.

Well, Ma says, we'll just have to get you some new ones.

I say, I need em for Gym tomorrow.

Ma rubs her face and says, What about your old pair? The ones with the big laces?

You threw em out, I say.

I did?

Yeah. I wanted to keep em but you said they stunk. I can't play dodgeball in my Sunday shoes.

Ma says, Maybe Shay has an old pair you can use.

Her foot's bigger than mine, I say. Coach Corcoran'll make me play in my socks.

Well, you'll have to make do until we can afford another pair, okay?

I say, Okay.

Then we are quiet. You can hear a car alarm going off somewhere in the distance.

I finish my eggs and Ma starts rubbing her eyes. When she's tired she rubs them so much it's like she's got an allergy.

After a minute I say, So is Al in prison?

Ma says, No, Blacky, he's not in prison.

Where is he? I ask.

He's in police custody.

Is that like jail?

She says, I'd rather not talk about it right now.

Before I take my plate to the sink Ma reaches her hand up and puts it on my cheek. Her fingers are warm and moist.

She says, School tomorrow, huh?

I nod.

Then she kisses my hair and goes back to her room.

She left the refrigerator open when she put the eggs back but I don't tell her this.

I will close it as soon as she shuts her door.

When we go to bed Cheedle falls asleep before me. I figure his brain must get tired from being a genius.

A major problem with me is that I have this thing about the dark. If the lights are out and Cheedle falls asleep before me I feel like I'm going to drown in my bed. It's a peculiar problem. There could be anyone in the room with me. It could even be a baby. If they're awake when I'm awake I'm okay. But as soon as I hear them sleeping I start to panic. This happened a couple of times with Tayshawn Van. Ma would come in to get him and I'd start to panic as soon as the door closed.

Hey, Cheedle, I say.

But he has already gone under. I can tell by his breathing.

Hey, Cheedle, I say again, but it's no use, so I get out of bed and climb the ladder and stare at him in the top bunk.

There's something perfect about Cheedle. Our black hair

looks better on him. Like it's meant to be black. Mine looks like a mistake.

I shake Cheedle's shoulder and he opens his eyes.

Hey, I say.

He says, Hey.

I just stare at him. His eyes are so big they look like Ma traded his regular ones for the eyes of a stuffed animal. I know he has a hard time focusing without his glasses. I wonder if he can see me at all.

What do you want? he asks.

I want to teach you how to kiss, I say.

Oh, he says. Interesting.

So open your mouth, I tell him.

Cheedle opens his mouth and then I put my lips on his.

We don't move.

His spit tastes clean and sweet.

I pretend it's Mandy Valentine's mouth and I press a little harder. Mandy Valentine's in my Social Studies class and she has the biggest breasts in the sixth grade. Once I had a dream that she unscrewed them and threw them into traffic. I woke up with a sharp need to urinate.

After a minute I take my mouth off.

That's how you kiss, I say.

Okay, he says.

So don't forget it.

I won't, he says.

Then I continue staring at him. I want to kiss him again

LORETTE WILMOT LIBRARY
NAZARETH COLLEGE

but I feel something cold and small turning in my stomach. I almost throw up but I make fists and swallow hard.

Go back to bed, Cheedle says.

I feel too slow for my own good.

He adds, If you're scared I might recommend reading *Anna Karenina*. You can use my booklight.

Then he closes his eyes and falls back to sleep like nothing happened.

In the bottom bunk I use Cheedle's light and start to read. After a few minutes I put the book back under the bed cause the names of the characters are too long and I keep getting stuck trying to picture what they look like.

Every time I close my eyes my head starts spinning.

Al Johnson's face is bigger than a pumpkin.

I get out of bed and go knock on Shay's door.

I think maybe I heard her come home while I was reading. Our house is very small and you can practically hear everything.

Once Shay punched the wall and made a hole. When Ma told Al Johnson he laughed and said, Pretty good for a girl. Then he put stuff in the hole and it got hard like cement. Ma was supposed to paint it white to match the rest of the wall but she never got around to it. Now it just sits there on the wall like an eye.

After Shay punched the wall Ma grounded her for three days. When Ma walked away Shay said, Fuckin walls are made of toilet paper.

Shay doesn't answer so I knock again.

After a minute I open the door.

Her curtains are blue and sluggish-looking. I figure she's in Rockdale smoking marijuana and fooling around with those skateboard guys who have the pierced faces.

Ma tries talking to her about stuff but Shay says she's got her own rules. I wish they would get along better.

Once we went bowling at the Galaxy Lanes on Jefferson Street and things seemed okay. Ma and Shay kept laughing cause they both threw nothing but gutter balls. Cheedle brought a book to read but even he bowled. He had to use both hands and he acted very serious. Every time he finished his frame he would go right back to reading.

A few weeks later I tried to get everyone to go bowling again but nobody had time.

Ma said, Maybe next month, Blacky.

Shay said, I got too much goin on right now.

Besides, it made my arm so sore, Ma added.

It was like they forgot how much fun it was.

Shay's room smells like cigarettes and air freshener. Her dresser drawers are hanging wide open so I go and close them. It's funny how there are very few clothes inside. I think it's cause most of them are scattered all over the floor.

I look in her closet for gym shoes but all that's in there are a pair of old black combat boots and empty packs of Kool cigarettes.

After I leave Shay's room I decide to go outside and get some air.

When you walk through the living room the floor creaks like a funhouse. I'm convinced that this is somehow related to the toilet paper walls.

You can hear the power meter buzzing on the side of the house. You used to be able to hear crickets, too. During the summer sometimes you can't tell what's the power meter and what's crickets.

Considering the hail I think it's pretty gutsy for the bugs to be out.

I walk around to the back of the house. There's a bunch of weeds growing near the hose hookup. Once I found a dead bird there. Its leg was twisted and something had bitten its head off.

A few days later I had a dream that the bird had my head and I could fly.

The moon looks small and sewn to the sky.

The backyard grass looks like hair. When I get strong enough Ma wants me to start using the hand mower.

Till then we'll just let it go, she says.

Till my body grows I will be thin and wimpish.

Sometimes I think I must have cancer cause I have very few muscles. Ma says I get that from my dad. He was small when he was little, too, she says.

But then he grew big enough so he could break stuff.

Including Ma's hand, which happened twice.

Once he did it by smashing it in the silverware drawer. Ma had to wear a cast and Cheedle and Shay and me signed it a hundred million times.

The leaves on the poplar tree are almost all gone now. I wonder if the hail has anything to do with this fact. I look for the cat from this morning but he's not there.

The swing set was put up when we were kids. It's orange with patches of rust. The swings are missing and now Ma uses it to beat the rugs. We have one rug in the kitchen and one in the bathroom. Currently the rug from the bathroom is hanging over it. It looks droopy and sad. It's supposed to be yellow but it's sort of green now.

Ma uses my old Wiffle ball bat to beat them. Whenever she comes back in the house she seems lost and out of breath.

Once after beating the rug from the kitchen she went straight down to the basement and didn't come up for the rest of the night. When I checked on her she was sitting on the floor, holding her wedding dress. I think she pulled it out of a box.

Hey, I said.

It was like she was sitting in a puddle.

She said, Hi, honey.

You okay? I asked.

I'm fine, she said. Go back upstairs, okay?

There are all sorts of things in those boxes in the basement. Once I found some pills in a little orange bottle. I showed Shay and she said they were Ma's and that they were for depression and mental illness but that Ma stopped taking them cause they were making her butt big. Shay said, Vain bitch should keep takin em.

I'm in front of Ma's window now and the breeze is making her curtains flutter.

Ma, I say to her, everything's gonna be okay, okay?

It surprises me how loud your voice can get when no one's listening.

We'll go bowling and stuff, I say.

The house next door is even smaller than ours. Mrs. Bunton lives there and she's got a poodle named Pierce that she talks to like it's human. She's so old I sometimes think she's a walking dead person.

You can see little bits of hail on Ma's windowsill.

Her bed is so huge it makes her look small like Cheedle. Her creams are still on her stomach and I worry that she'll roll over and squish them.

Ma, I say again, but she can't hear me cause she's asleep.

She forgot to take her clothes off and she's still wearing her shoes.

In school I feel like people can see inside me. Like all my veins and tissues.

In Life Science I sit behind Anne Meadows. Her hair is so blond it makes you wonder about stuff. In Art I have tried to paint this hair several times but I never get it right.

I always make the hair without a head cause I don't know how to paint faces yet. Al Johnson taught me how to draw them with charcoal pencils but using a brush is much more difficult.

Soon you'll do faces, Miss Haze told me after class one day. That's the next step, Blacky. Faces.

Anne Meadows' hair always winds up looking like wood or clothes. Or it's too orange cause I don't mix the paints right.

Once Miss Haze asked me what it was and I told her it was hay.

Nice effort, she said. Keep trying, Blacky.

Anne Meadows has a box for her pens and pencils and I admire her organizational skills.

I also admire the fact that she wears Ralph Lauren shirts and smells like Clairol Herbal Essences shampoo.

I have written Anne Meadows this note. I carry it around in my pocket every day. I often take it out to check and recheck it for spelling and grammar errors.

I am happy to say that it is an error-free note.

It says:

> *Anne,*
>
> *May I have your phone number? I would enjoy discussing various subjects with you. I have time if you have time.*
>
> *Sincerely,*
> *Blacky Brown*

I saw her looking at me once. She was making a face like she was hungry. I shared this with my good friend Eric Duggan and he said she probably was hungry and not to get too excited.

I have been tempted a million times to drop this note in her box.

It's hard being a coward. It makes you wonder when you will grow out of it.

Is it a body thing or a mind thing?

Suddenly Mr. Prisby asks me if I can repeat what *thoracic* means.

When I open my mouth I have to close it right away cause I have this feeling that my teeth are going to fall out.

I don't know, I say. What is it?

He looks at me for a moment and shakes his head.

Then he says, John, do you know?

John Sellers says, It means of, relating to, located in, or involving the thorax.

John Sellers has perfect hair and carries a Palm Pilot M500 in his pocket. I see him using it often and I'm sure he will go far in life.

Did you catch that? Mr. Prisby asks me.

Yes, I say.

He says, You know where the thorax is, right, Blacky?

The throat, I say.

I don't realize that I'm touching my throat when I say it.

Please pay attention, Blacky, Mr. Prisby says to me.

Sorry, I say.

There's a see-through fake human standing next to the chalkboard. You can see his organs. Mr. Prisby calls him Dave and often pretends to speak to him, and the girls on the left side of the room always laugh.

He'll say, What's a herbivore, Dave?

He'll say, Hey, Dave, I forgot my lunch money, wanna lend me five bucks?

Everyone laughs cause Mr. Prisby is a master of comedy and he has been known to give extra credit to the ones who laugh the most.

When the passing period tone sounds, Mr. Prisby asks if he can have a word with me.

Blacky, he says, may I have a word with you?

One of the girls from the left side of the room makes a face like she is going to laugh.

I approach Mr. Prisby's desk.

He wears glasses with black frames. The lenses are so thick they make his eyes look far away.

He looks up at me with his hands in a triangle.

Is everything okay, Blacky? he asks.

Yes, I say.

Are you sure?

I'm sure, I say.

You seem like you're in outer space today.

I'm not, I say.

I'd really like to see you bring that C up to a B in here.

I will, I say.

I'd like that very much.

Me too.

And I'm sure your mother would.

I nod.

Then Mr. Prisby says, I think you have a lot of potential, Blacky.

Oh, I say. Thanks.

Teachers talk about potential like it's a jar of pennies.

He says, Your paper on the cats in New York City was quite thorough. I was very impressed with it.

lon't wanna see any monkeys out there, he warns.

en he blows the whistle and everyone goes for the five
in the middle. I never go for them cause you usually get
ughly pummeled at close range by Steve Degerald or
Keefler. Today I make an extra-special effort not to go
e balls cause I don't have any gym shoes and it's diffi-
) run and stop when you're in your socks.

rmally I would fake it by running a few steps and then
ck up and cling to the bleacher wall.

c Duggan squeezes in next to me and says, I have some
sting information regarding the Abominable Snowman.

c Duggan has recently become my good friend. This
ned cause I helped him find his glasses after they got
ed off when we were playing flag football.

icked them up out of the dirt just before they got
ed.

en I handed them to him he said, I owe you one,
 I owe you big.

e that day he will often pay for my hot lunch and he
 use his Language Arts textbook cause I left mine in
ia when we were visiting Ma's dead sister, Aunt Diana.

ugh cable television Eric Duggan has gathered quite
 interesting knowledge about various subjects that he
 share.

about sharks and their predatory habits.

 the names and colors of poisonous snakes in
a.

Thanks, I say again.

I'd hate to see you lose that momentum.

Me too, I say.

My paper focused on three cats in New York City who
jumped out of windows due to urban stress. One of them
landed on a gate and was fatally punctured. His name was
Socks and he was a Blue Russian.

Mr. Prisby starts playing with a pencil.

I just stand there like Dave the See-Through Fake
Human. I wonder if he ever feels ashamed for not having
any skin or clothes.

Mr. Prisby says, How are you feeling, Blacky?

I say, I'm okay.

You look a little faint.

I'm fine, I say.

Is everything okay at home?

Yes.

Let's concentrate a little better in class, okay?

I say, Okay.

Very good then, he says. I have to set up the film projector
for my next class.

He gets up and crosses to the back of the room.

I want to move but I feel stuck again.

You better get to your next period, Mr. Prisby says, his
back to me now.

Okay, I say.

I have to hit myself in the thigh to get my legs to move.

While he's setting up the film projector I reach into Dave the See-Through Fake Human's mouth and take out his tongue.

I don't know why I do this. I have nothing against Mr. Prisby or Dave the See-Through Fake Human either. My hand just sort of does it on its own.

The tongue feels cold and useless in my palm.

I am tempted to take a kidney or a lung too, but that would be too obvious, so I put the tongue in my pocket and leave.

In Gym we play dodgeball.

Like usual the sides get split up unevenly.

Steve Degerald and Evan Keefler are on the same team. I am not on that team and this means pain.

Steve Degerald shaves his head and pretends he is in the Marines. He'll sometimes shout Semper Fi! for no reason. Once he did it in Language Arts in the middle of an SRA test. Semper Fi! he shouted and threw his fists in the air. Miss Cosgrove looked up but nothing happened.

Last month he walked up to me in the hall and said, I'm gonna stab you someday, Brown.

I said, Why?

Cause you're weaker than a girl and that makes you a toad. All toads need to be eliminated.

I have never done anything to deserve this but that's the way it is with Steve Degerald.

He is such a superior athlete that he can catch a dodgeball

with one hand and throw it back
Sometimes he throws it so hard it ma
He's got huge arms and hair on his t

I know this word cause Mr. Prisb
in Life Science.

These are Dave's testicles, he sa
area. Testicles are the male re
continued. They're also known as te

There are only a couple of kids
have hair on their testicles and S
them.

Evan Keefler's got hair on hi
nothing to brag about. It looks mor
testicle hair. It's so straight I imag
comb.

The trick to dodgeball is you hav
throw it and pummel the other te

I wanna see some good play o
Corcoran says while setting the
Strategy and team play!

He smiles and his teeth are sh

Before the game starts all play
one part of their body touching
rule that is enforced at all costs.
you cheating there are pushups
Monkey Drill is where you run
the lines on the basketball court

I
T
balls
thor
Evan
for t
cult
N
I'd b
Er
intere
Er
happ
knoc
I
stom
W
Black
Sin
lets m
Centr
Th
a lot o
likes t
Lik
An
Austra

What information? I ask him.

The Sherpas referred to the Abominable Snowman as The Man Who Is Not a Man, Eric Duggan says.

Who are the Sherpas? I ask.

This tribe of people from Nepal. Some British explorers in the nineteenth century saw him in the Himalayas. Their records indicate that he was eight and a half feet tall. Hair all over his body. Wide shoulders. Apelike face. They said he could disappear.

Wow, I say.

Eric Duggan lives on the other side of town where the houses have tree forts and swimming pools.

Once when I was at his house he gave me one of his X-Games Big Air BMX bikes so we could ride through Hamil Woods together. It was black with yellow mags. We were going to set up a ramp and jump the creek but we couldn't find the right size piece of plywood. Instead of jumping the creek he taught me how to do a bronco and a wheelie.

When I went to give it back to him he said, Keep it.

I said, Really?

Yeah, he said. You can have it. I got three other ones.

It was a world-class style bike but my Ma made me give it back cause she has a rule about charity.

But Ma, I pleaded, he's got four of em!

She said, People just expect stuff from you when they start giving you things. We don't accept charity, Blacky, and that's that.

Eric Duggan says, The Sherpas believed the Abominable Snowman was a time traveler. It was on the Discovery Channel last night. They did a segment on Bigfoot, too. Great Beast Myths. You gotta check that program out, Blacky. Fascinating stuff.

We don't get that channel, I explain.

He says, I thought you had cable.

We do, I say, but it's only Basic.

Eric Duggan says, Oh, and pulls his socks up. They have two green stripes each. He has many variations of gym socks and I admire this fact.

So where were you yesterday? he asks, adjusting the band that keeps his glasses on his head.

He's standing next to me and touching the bleacher wall with his heel.

I tell Eric Duggan that I was at the hospital.

I had to go to the hospital, I say.

Are you sick or something? Eric Duggan asks.

I get that ache in my chest again, so I say, I got stabbed.

You did?

Yes.

Cool, he says. Where?

In the hip, I say. I was at the mall and this guy jumped me next to Caramel Corn Forever. It's a very minor stab wound but he got my Nikes.

It hurts me to lie to Eric Duggan. It feels like there's a fist in my stomach.

Thanks, I say again.

I'd hate to see you lose that momentum.

Me too, I say.

My paper focused on three cats in New York City who jumped out of windows due to urban stress. One of them landed on a gate and was fatally punctured. His name was Socks and he was a Blue Russian.

Mr. Prisby starts playing with a pencil.

I just stand there like Dave the See-Through Fake Human. I wonder if he ever feels ashamed for not having any skin or clothes.

Mr. Prisby says, How are you feeling, Blacky?

I say, I'm okay.

You look a little faint.

I'm fine, I say.

Is everything okay at home?

Yes.

Let's concentrate a little better in class, okay?

I say, Okay.

Very good then, he says. I have to set up the film projector for my next class.

He gets up and crosses to the back of the room.

I want to move but I feel stuck again.

You better get to your next period, Mr. Prisby says, his back to me now.

Okay, I say.

I have to hit myself in the thigh to get my legs to move.

While he's setting up the film projector I reach into Dave the See-Through Fake Human's mouth and take out his tongue.

I don't know why I do this. I have nothing against Mr. Prisby or Dave the See-Through Fake Human either. My hand just sort of does it on its own.

The tongue feels cold and useless in my palm.

I am tempted to take a kidney or a lung too, but that would be too obvious, so I put the tongue in my pocket and leave.

In Gym we play dodgeball.

Like usual the sides get split up unevenly.

Steve Degerald and Evan Keefler are on the same team. I am not on that team and this means pain.

Steve Degerald shaves his head and pretends he is in the Marines. He'll sometimes shout Semper Fi! for no reason. Once he did it in Language Arts in the middle of an SRA test. Semper Fi! he shouted and threw his fists in the air. Miss Cosgrove looked up but nothing happened.

Last month he walked up to me in the hall and said, I'm gonna stab you someday, Brown.

I said, Why?

Cause you're weaker than a girl and that makes you a toad. All toads need to be eliminated.

I have never done anything to deserve this but that's the way it is with Steve Degerald.

He is such a superior athlete that he can catch a dodgeball

with one hand and throw it back in the same motion. Sometimes he throws it so hard it makes the bleachers echo. He's got huge arms and hair on his testicles.

I know this word cause Mr. Prisby taught it to us one day in Life Science.

These are Dave's testicles, he said, pointing to the nut area. Testicles are the male reproductive organs, he continued. They're also known as testes.

There are only a couple of kids in the sixth grade who have hair on their testicles and Steve Degerald is one of them.

Evan Keefler's got hair on his testicles, too, but it's nothing to brag about. It looks more like mustache hair than testicle hair. It's so straight I imagine him styling it with a comb.

The trick to dodgeball is you have to get the ball so you can throw it and pummel the other team.

I wanna see some good play out there today, boys! Coach Corcoran says while setting the balls on the midcourt line. Strategy and team play!

He smiles and his teeth are sharp and gray.

Before the game starts all players on each side must have one part of their body touching the bleacher wall. This is a rule that is enforced at all costs. If Coach Corcoran catches you cheating there are pushups and the Monkey Drill. The Monkey Drill is where you run back and forth and touch all the lines on the basketball court.

I don't wanna see any monkeys out there, he warns.

Then he blows the whistle and everyone goes for the five balls in the middle. I never go for them cause you usually get thoroughly pummeled at close range by Steve Degerald or Evan Keefler. Today I make an extra-special effort not to go for the balls cause I don't have any gym shoes and it's difficult to run and stop when you're in your socks.

Normally I would fake it by running a few steps and then I'd back up and cling to the bleacher wall.

Eric Duggan squeezes in next to me and says, I have some interesting information regarding the Abominable Snowman.

Eric Duggan has recently become my good friend. This happened cause I helped him find his glasses after they got knocked off when we were playing flag football.

I picked them up out of the dirt just before they got stomped.

When I handed them to him he said, I owe you one, Blacky. I owe you big.

Since that day he will often pay for my hot lunch and he lets me use his Language Arts textbook cause I left mine in Centralia when we were visiting Ma's dead sister, Aunt Diana.

Through cable television Eric Duggan has gathered quite a lot of interesting knowledge about various subjects that he likes to share.

Like about sharks and their predatory habits.

And the names and colors of poisonous snakes in Australia.

What information? I ask him.

The Sherpas referred to the Abominable Snowman as The Man Who Is Not a Man, Eric Duggan says.

Who are the Sherpas? I ask.

This tribe of people from Nepal. Some British explorers in the nineteenth century saw him in the Himalayas. Their records indicate that he was eight and a half feet tall. Hair all over his body. Wide shoulders. Apelike face. They said he could disappear.

Wow, I say.

Eric Duggan lives on the other side of town where the houses have tree forts and swimming pools.

Once when I was at his house he gave me one of his X-Games Big Air BMX bikes so we could ride through Hamil Woods together. It was black with yellow mags. We were going to set up a ramp and jump the creek but we couldn't find the right size piece of plywood. Instead of jumping the creek he taught me how to do a bronco and a wheelie.

When I went to give it back to him he said, Keep it.

I said, Really?

Yeah, he said. You can have it. I got three other ones.

It was a world-class style bike but my Ma made me give it back cause she has a rule about charity.

But Ma, I pleaded, he's got four of em!

She said, People just expect stuff from you when they start giving you things. We don't accept charity, Blacky, and that's that.

Eric Duggan says, The Sherpas believed the Abominable Snowman was a time traveler. It was on the Discovery Channel last night. They did a segment on Bigfoot, too. Great Beast Myths. You gotta check that program out, Blacky. Fascinating stuff.

We don't get that channel, I explain.

He says, I thought you had cable.

We do, I say, but it's only Basic.

Eric Duggan says, Oh, and pulls his socks up. They have two green stripes each. He has many variations of gym socks and I admire this fact.

So where were you yesterday? he asks, adjusting the band that keeps his glasses on his head.

He's standing next to me and touching the bleacher wall with his heel.

I tell Eric Duggan that I was at the hospital.

I had to go to the hospital, I say.

Are you sick or something? Eric Duggan asks.

I get that ache in my chest again, so I say, I got stabbed.

You did?

Yes.

Cool, he says. Where?

In the hip, I say. I was at the mall and this guy jumped me next to Caramel Corn Forever. It's a very minor stab wound but he got my Nikes.

It hurts me to lie to Eric Duggan. It feels like there's a fist in my stomach.

Who was the guy? he asks.

I don't know, I say. I think he was Native American, though.

Eric Duggan says, Whoa.

In Social Studies we're taught to call Indians Native Americans. Miss Cosgrove is very stern about such matters.

Asian, not Oriental, she says.

African American, not black.

Once Charles Vershaw stood up and screamed Nigger! I guess he couldn't take it anymore.

They put him in the Quiet Room and now he sees Dr. Lockwood on a weekly basis. Dr. Lockwood is the school guidance counselor and when you get called into his office it's usually cause you've had a mental breakdown.

Coach Corcoran blows his whistle and everyone sprints for the five dodgeballs. I run about ten feet and retreat back to the wall of bleachers. I have to slide and this will not be good for my dodging technique.

There is some extreme pummeling at the midcourt line and then both sides prepare for the strategy and team play part.

Bill Mann and Robert Kinsella hurl balls at us. They make hate faces and their eyes go small.

This is what it's like to be hunted by the enemy, I think.

Bill Mann's ball sails over my head and slams into the bleachers. Robert Kinsella's ball hits Eric Duggan in the face and his glasses fly. Eric Duggan sits down like he's tired. His left lens has popped out and that eye looks huge and glued on.

Robert Kinsella makes a power fist like he won the Illinois Lotto.

Eric Duggan stands up but he has to sit down again. And then he farts and makes a face.

They'll no doubt be talking about this in the cafeteria.

When I go to help him Steve Degerald throws a ball and it hits me square in the chest. The sound is like meat falling on the kitchen floor. I slip a little but I keep from falling.

It feels like I've walked into a mailbox.

My breath goes away for a second and I cough.

Sometimes I worry that my lungs are too small.

I sit like Eric Duggan but I don't get back up. Generally I do my best to not be stupid.

I don't want them talking about me in the cafeteria.

Steve Degerald is holding two balls now. He's looking at me and pretending they're breasts. Evan Keefler can't get enough of this and he laughs like a witch.

Someday I will grow large and wield certain weapons. Like nunchucks or those swords from *Blackbelt Theater*.

You're out, Brown, Coach Corcoran says. And you too, Duggan.

Eric Duggan finally finds his lens and we move off to the side. Half of his face is pink and he's doing his best not to touch it.

It takes Eric Duggan too long to make his way to the side

and Coach Corcoran isn't pleased about this fact.

When you're out you're out! Coach Corcoran yells. If you can't play by the rules then you won't play at all! You two get a shower!

We can't do the Monkey Drill today cause the girls are on the other side of the gym playing badminton.

Coach Corcoran is old and has a face that looks like it is made out of bread and everyone knows he fought in the Vietnam Conflict.

In Social Studies Miss Cosgrove corrected Heidi Winch when she called Vietnam a war.

It was a *conflict*, Heidi, Miss Cosgrove said. This country hasn't fought in a war in a very long time.

Coach Corcoran has tattoos and he tries to hide them by wearing long sleeves but they always creep up his forearms.

One of the tattoos is a woman with large breasts and a snake.

Next week we got the Presidential Physical Fitness Test, Coach Corcoran says. You better find those shoes, Brown, or I'd advise getting a new pair.

At the end of the fifth grade I caught Coach Corcoran picking his nose. He rolled the snots between his fingers and stared at it. He saw me watching him and I'm convinced that this is why he takes a special interest in me.

In the shower Eric Duggan is still trying not to touch his face. His body is thin and blank like mine. His penis looks like a mushroom.

While showering I always worry that I will pop a boner, but the water is cold and this helps matters.

Coach Corcoran has a three-minute rule and even though he's not here to enforce it we play along cause everyone in the sixth grade believes that his experience in the Vietnam Conflict gave him special powers.

So did you see the hail yesterday? Eric Duggan asks, putting his pits under the water.

I saw it, I say.

Pretty weird, huh? Hail in October?

It *is* weird, I say.

Eric Duggan says, Mr. Prisby said it's the first hail he's seen in over ten years.

I have no idea why we're talking about hail. The fact that everyone keeps bringing it up must mean something.

I imagine spaceships coming down and taking people away.

The cuts on my feet still sting. Ma left some Neosporin antibacterial ointment for me on the kitchen table but after I put it on most of it got smeared in my sock.

Eric Duggan touches his face and then his lip starts to quiver. He's been trying to make his lip stop quivering for several minutes now.

His nipples are so small they're like mosquito bites. You practically have to do detective work to find them.

You okay? I ask Eric Duggan.

Don't touch me! he says.

I don't realize I'm touching him till I'm doing it. My hand is on his cheek where the ball hit him. He's looking at me like I'm part werewolf.

I don't like to be touched, he says, and backs away from his water spray. He puts a fist in front of his testicles and looks at me all over.

You didn't get stabbed, he says, pointing at my hip with his free hand.

I know, I say.

You lied to me.

His eyes go small and hard.

That ache in my chest is crawling up my throat. I swallow hard and say, I'm sorry.

But he just keeps standing there so I say it again. I say, I'm sorry, Eric.

And what's wrong with your feet, anyway? he asks.

I say, I lost my Nikes in the woods. They're just irritated.

What were you doing in the woods? he asks.

Just running around, I say.

By yourself?

I was with my sister, I explain. We were looking for leaves to press. I'm sorry I lied, Eric.

I realize that I am piling lies on top of lies. This fact makes my ears feel like they're burning.

When we are dressing Eric asks me if I'm a faggot.

Are you a faggot or something? he asks.

No, I say.

Then stop staring at my dick, he says.

We are quiet while we dress. You can hear dodgeballs slamming into the bleachers.

By the way, Eric Duggan says suddenly, I hope you realize you've been wearing those pants for three days in a row.

All my other ones are dirty, I explain.

If you need extra pants just tell me, he says. I have several spare pairs.

Okay.

You have to minimize your skankiness, he tells me. There's nothing worse than skank.

I think about how on the average I don't consider these things enough. Ma gets busy and forgets to do laundry. We have a washer and dryer in the basement but the washer started doing stuff to our clothes. Once they came out with big white spots all over them. Now Ma does the laundry at this place on Plainfield Road. It's got candy machines and a thing that makes quarters.

Eric Duggan says, Let's go to lunch. They got pizza pockets today.

On our way to the cafeteria Eric Duggan stops in the hall and shows me the new Beck CD. Beck looks bored and invincible. After he puts the jewel box back in his backpack I tell him about what happened with Al Johnson.

I'm not sure why I choose this time to tell him.

I think it's cause of that ache in my throat. I made it go down to my chest but now it's creeping back up.

The incident comes out so fast it makes me feel like everything around us is moving backwards.

When I get to the part about Al Johnson's thumb in my butt it feels like my head might pop off again. There's even a moment when I put my hand on the top of my skull to keep this from happening. I almost start to cry but I flex my arms as hard as I can and this helps.

Jesus, Eric Duggan says. Holy shit, man.

We are standing in front of the boys' bathroom now and it makes me want to urinate.

Eric Duggan won't blink and I think this must be a positive thing. I notice that he's fitted his lens back in his glasses but there is a thumbprint in the middle.

I'm glad I've told Eric Duggan the truth. I am relieved.

Ma always says, No matter how hard it is you gotta tell the truth, Blacky. No matter how hard.

Some kids from Gym are coming down the hall.

It's Robert Kinsella and Bill Mann. Bill Mann's hair is wet and combed to perfection.

Eric Duggan just stands there like he doesn't know what to do.

I say, What?

He opens his mouth like he's going to say something but nothing comes out.

Sorry, I say. Sorry, Eric.

When Robert Kinsella and Bill Mann walk by they are performing a rap song. Robert Kinsella rhymes and flails his arms. Bill Mann beatboxes into his fists. His shirt is so red it looks soaked in blood.

Eric Duggan says, I gotta wash my hands.

Okay, I say.

See you, he says.

I say, See you later.

Then Eric Duggan walks into the boys' bathroom.

I want to follow him but I don't.

I can almost feel that ache in my mouth now.

6

At lunch I walk up to Eric Duggan at our table. He's sitting with Jonas Kelser, this kid who doesn't have a telephone in his house.

I know this fact about Jonas Kelser cause on the first day of school, in Speech, Drama, and Journalism, Miss Williams made everyone stand up and talk for two minutes about a gift they wanted for Christmas and why.

I said I wanted a pit bull for protection.

Roger Rebillard said he wanted a Jet Ski for his daredevil lifestyle.

Jonas Kelser said he wanted a telephone cause all he had was a pay phone on the corner.

Hey, I say to Eric Duggan.

What's up? he says.

Hey, Jonas, I say.

Jonas says, Hey, Blacky, and looks down at his plate. He

has a cowlick and big bulging eyes.

Can I sit with you guys? I say.

Eric Duggan says, We're sort of having a meeting, right, Jonas?

Yes, Jonas says, still looking down at his plate.

A meeting about what? I say.

Eric Duggan says, Just a meeting, and wipes his spork with a napkin.

They are both eating pizza rolls with assorted vegetables.

I want to ask Eric Duggan for money so I can get a pizza roll too, but there's something about the way he's not looking at me.

What's wrong? I say to Eric Duggan.

What? he says. What?

But he still won't look at me, so I walk over to the other side of the cafeteria.

The tables are all completely full except for Mary Jane Paddington's, so I go over by her.

Mary Jane Paddington is an unusual person who likes to eat alone. She hardly ever speaks and I don't think she has a single friend.

This might be cause she wears the same clothes a lot. Or cause she dyed her pants red after she ran out of Language Arts with her menstrual blood leaking through her crotch.

Before that happened her pants were white and everyone knows they're the same pants.

Those are the same pants, I heard Tonya Ellis telling

Lynnette Collins under her breath. They were in the hallway during a passing period.

Mary Jane Paddington walked right by them and they watched her like she was part animal.

Lynnette Collins said, Who's she trying to fool?

Mary Jane Paddington's glasses are a little crooked sometimes. And she doesn't comb her hair much either. Eric Duggan told me she has a pet rat and feeds it fingernails. Evan Keefler calls her Wolf Girl cause she's got these eyes. They are so yellow they look like science fiction.

Some people say she's got scabies.

Others say she's got a nest of spiders in her hair.

These are obviously false rumors spread by all those girls in the eighth grade who have identical haircuts. There's about ten in this group and once they came to school wearing the exact same thing. Light blue shirts and black pants. Everyone said it was a miracle.

They got so excited that they went into the Student Council room and had the photo editor of the yearbook take a picture.

Some of those same girls refer to each other by their email addresses.

Hey, Toasty Tina.

Hey, Jenny two twenty-four.

What's up, T-Bone Salad?

Blue Babe, where were you last night? We were chatting up a storm!

It can go on and on.

Across the cafeteria Eric Duggan is looking at me like I'm a shark or a monkey. He even points at me and says something to Jonas Kelser.

Mary Jane Paddington is eating Fritos and a tuna sandwich. She eats so slow it's like she's got frostbite.

Hey, I say.

Hey, she says without looking up.

I can tell she's not impressed by much. Her hair is black with streaks of red. I imagine it's this way on purpose.

Can I sit here? I ask.

Sure, she says, still looking down.

I can see that one of her lenses is scratched. This is unfortunate and it makes her left eye look diseased.

At the edge of the cafeteria there's a rectangle of tiles that don't match the rest of the floor. These tiles are gray and the others are white with specks. Everyone calls this rectangle of gray tiles the Paddington Pit and when people leave the cafeteria they jump over it like it's infested with AIDS.

I must admit that I did this once.

While in the air I didn't feel any safer. I actually felt like I might get hurt.

Why are you sitting here? Mary Jane Paddington asks, finally looking up.

There's nowhere else to sit, I say.

You could sit over by Eric Duggan and Jonas Kelser, she says.

No, I can't, I say.

She says, But you always sit with Eric Duggan.

I say, I can't today.

How come?

Cause he's having an important meeting, I say.

She is wearing a long-sleeved T-shirt with a picture of a duck on it. The duck is saying QUACK OFF, MOTHERQUACKER!

The noise in the cafeteria is like computers running. It's funny how voices can sound like machines.

I stare at her tuna sandwich. The crusts have been cut off and there are bits of celery mixed in with the tuna.

So sit, Mary Jane Paddington says. You're only making everyone look at you more.

I stand there for another second. I can feel eyes on my neck like bugs.

Sit, I command myself with the voice in my head. Sit, Blacky.

I sit down across from her.

Mary Jane Paddington is eating each Frito one corner at a time. I note that this is a very peculiar way to eat Fritos. Her mouth looks like it hurts when she chews.

Did you do your Social Studies homework? she asks.

No, I say. I wasn't in school yesterday.

I noticed, she says. Where were you?

I was sick, I say. What was the assignment?

We were supposed to write a one-page essay about our thoughts on capital punishment.

Oh.

I wrote two. You can have one of mine if you'd like.

I say, Thanks. Why'd you write two?

I had a lot to say about it, she says. Then she eats another Frito.

Look, I say, and put the tongue on the table.

What is that? she asks.

It's Dave the See-Through Fake Human's tongue. I stole it from Life Science when Mr. Prisby wasn't looking.

What are you gonna do with it? she asks.

I don't know, I say. Carry it around, I guess.

You should put it in a Ziploc bag and send it to him in the mail.

Oh, I say. Why?

Keep him on his toes, she says. Teachers gotta learn stuff, too.

Huh, I say.

I wonder if she and Cheedle have been spending time together.

We eat our lunch and we are quiet.

I look over at Eric Duggan again. He's got his arm around Jonas Kelser like there's valuable information to know about his side of the cafeteria.

When Mary Jane Paddington is finished eating her lunch she opens her backpack and removes the essay about capital punishment. She slides it across the table to me.

Make sure to copy it over, she says. Miss Cosgrove knows my handwriting.

Thanks, I say. Can I fold it up?

She says, You can do whatever you want with it. Just don't put it in a Ziploc bag and send it to me in the mail.

I know this is supposed to be a joke but I don't get it.

Cheedle would get it.

Shay would probably get it, too.

I smile anyway. My face feels heavy and tired.

It's raining so hard it looks like the window is melting.

I am in Social Studies for sixth period. They give you four extra passing minutes between fifth and sixth period so you can exchange books at your locker. According to the Student Handbook this is the first year they've instituted this rule.

I usually walk around with Eric Duggan and discuss pertinent subjects that he's read about or seen on various cable television shows.

Like the effects of overpopulation in the ghettos.

Or blind kids in Malaysia who get paid ten cents an hour to make expensive American basketball shoes.

But he has Jonas Kelser now.

So I didn't go to my locker and came straight to Social Studies instead.

Miss Cosgrove is organizing her desk. She likes things nice and neat. Her hair is pulled back and twisted into a bun. She often wears clothes that look like they've been ordered out of a catalog. I enjoy smelling her cause she always wears a particular perfume.

Hello, Blacky, she says.

Hello, I say.

You're a bit early, aren't you?

Yes, I say.

No locker time?

Didn't need it, I say.

We missed you yesterday, she says, smoothing the front of her shirt. I can see her nipples and this makes my face hotter than usual.

Is everything okay? she asks.

Yes, I say. My voice cracks a little. This must have something to do with her nipples.

You sure?

Yes.

Are you feeling all right?

I'm not falling, I say.

She says, I didn't say you were.

We don't talk for a second. For some reason I imagine the kinds of things she keeps in the drawers of her desk.

Stuff like aspirin and little tissues. A secret bottle of perfume. A tube of lipstick.

Miss Cosgrove leans forward and says, I asked if you're *feel*ing all right, Blacky. *Feel*ing.

Oh, I say.

It's just that you seem so far away.

But I'm not.

She stops leaning so much and paperclips some forms.

She says, How's your mom doing these days?

I say, She's okay.

Is she still working at St. Joe's?

Yes.

Well, please tell her I say hello and give her my regards.

Okay.

Miss Cosgrove always wants to give her regards to people.

Like regards are little chocolates wrapped in foil.

She says, I look forward to seeing her at parent-teacher conferences.

I don't reply cause I know there will be lots of concern at this particular conference. Miss Cosgrove is always trying to recommend adjustments to my study habits. For state capitals she suggested that I use flash cards. I got only thirty-five of the state capitals correct, so she let me retake the test. I used the flash cards to study with, but I got only thirty-two correct the second time.

I worked hard on it, too.

The problem was I kept imagining myself getting lost in all those cities.

Like Montpelier, Vermont.

And Tallahassee, Florida.

Albany was a tough one, too. I couldn't ever seem to get out of Albany.

Miss Cosgrove has gone back to arranging her desk.

There are three polished stones on three stacks of papers.

I imagine her house. I see things stacked everywhere.

Plates and mail and stuff like that. Neat stacks with little polished stones on top. I picture her married to a mailman. He never takes off his uniform and when they have sex he just undoes his fly and they moan at each other like they're sad.

I take out Mary Jane Paddington's homework assignment about capital punishment. I begin copying it into my own notebook.

It reads:

> Capital punishment is horrendous. People make mistakes and they should be punished, but putting others to death is animalistic behavior. Another's death is not for us to decide. It's up to God to settle such matters of the mortal soul.
>
> I don't believe capital punishment solves anything. There's a guy named Mumia who is on Death Row in Philadelphia for killing a policeman in a race-related shootout. There is fishy evidence regarding this case. I wish they would free Mumia and go after the real evidence.

As I am copying Mary Jane Paddington's assignment, Evan Keefler and Steve Degerald pass by the doorway.

They see me and stop.

Steve Degerald points at me and gives me a thumbs-up.

Then Evan Keefler does the same.

They are grinning so hard it's like their teeth hurt.

I look away.

In the window the rain is coming harder. It's like someone is controlling it with a dial.

When I look back to the doorway Steve Degerald and Evan Keefler are gone.

In the bus line Jared Collins points at me and shoots me a thumbs-up.

Then Kevin Buhle and Richard Falcon do it too.

Richard Falcon's thumb has a black nail. In Language Arts I've seen him color it with a permanent marker. He calls it his Evil Thumb. He tells people he has tattoos but it's a lie. I know this cause I saw him in the Student Council room with all of his clothes off. I don't know why he was naked. He was all alone and sitting really still in one of the homeroom delegate chairs. I had missed my bus cause of a bathroom emergency. I walked into the Student Council room and there he was.

He didn't have a single tattoo.

It's funny how we create stories about our bodies.

For instance, the other day I heard Sean Maloney tell Coach Corcoran that he can't wear a jock cause he's got three testicles. In a few weeks the old woman with the lunchmeat face who works in the Health Office is going to come into the locker room and check all the sixth-grade boys for hernias. Rumor has it that she fondles you and makes you turn your head and cough. I'll be sure to listen for how many times Sean Maloney coughs.

When the bus leaders come around everyone files out to the parking lot and starts boarding their buses. The rain is coming down in a way that makes you want to ball up and get muscular.

The windshield wipers sound like dogs crying.

When it's my turn to board I hesitate.

Let's go, Blacky! the bus driver says.

Her eyes are small like a lizard's.

You're holding up the line, she yells. Let's go!

My tongue feels like it's shrinking.

I forgot something, I say.

Then I turn around and walk away from the line.

Janice Caulkoven and Ben Jansen are sharing an umbrella. It's so big it's even stopping the rain that's going sideways.

It's funny how never having an umbrella can make you feel left out.

I stop at the school doors and turn.

When buses start to move it's like they got their own imaginations.

For some reason I feel the need to wave goodbye to my bus, so I do.

I wave so hard my hand goes floppy.

As it pulls away I can see four thumbs framed in four different windows.

. . .

I walk home on Caton Farm Road cause the buses don't use it. There's a new subdivision going up and the rain makes the houses look like they were dropped out of the sky.

Nobody lives here yet. It's all piles of bricks and skeleton wood.

There is a yellow bulldozer parked in mud. The door is open so I go inside. This feels highly illegal but it is thrilling to be a smalltime criminal.

I imagine it takes special skill to operate a bulldozer cause the controls are all sticks and levers.

There is a black hardhat on the seat. I put it on and imagine myself playing dodgeball. I break all the rules and charge Steve Degerald and Evan Keefler with my head. They slam up against the bleachers and I can hear their ribs crack. I can almost feel their bones breaking in my teeth.

From the cab of the bulldozer I can see into the half-made house. It's all skinny wood and chicken wire. I think about how houses have bones too.

I wonder when they put the walls in cause the walls are skin.

I wonder how electricity works cause electricity's like veins. Trying to figure this out makes me sleepy.

My hair is soaked and so are the bottoms of my jeans.

I can smell my body. It's like meat with spices.

I doubt that this is a pleasant experience to inhale.

Ma says I don't need to start using deodorant yet but I think I do.

The bulldozer windshield is getting all steamy and I write a letter with my finger.

> Boy,
>> Where are you? I miss you.
>>> Girl

I see Al Johnson in jail.

They shave his head and beat him with sticks.

He falls to his knees and begs for mercy.

And then a guard with a gold tooth urinates on his skull.

My breath steams over the words on the windshield and my letter is gone.

I walk the rest of the way home.

You always hear about gang activity on this side of town. The Vicelords and the Latin Kings.

Watch out for the gangs, Blacky, Ma says sometimes. I guess Chicago isn't big enough for them.

You can tell who they are cause they cock their hats funny.

Eric Duggan said that once he was at Aladdin's Castle in the mall and a Vicelord walked up to him and made him remove his Cubs hat.

If they come after me I will hide in a dumpster.

I realize that I am still wearing the hardhat but I don't feel guilty and I keep it on.

The rain dies a little but not much.

I think about cutting through Hamil Woods. I could rest

in the dugout at the baseball field.

But you never know when the Smudge Man will come out of his hole.

I imagine meeting him.

Hello, Smudge Man, I say, nice to finally meet you.

He is gentle and scary at the same time.

He plays his violin and I get hypnotized.

Then he takes me down into his hole and eats my brain with a spoon.

By the time I get home, the rain has stopped and the back-yard looks like rubber.

Cheedle is under the swing set with his typewriter. He's sitting on newspapers and wearing a red football helmet. The helmet makes his head look huge.

Hey, I say.

He says, Hey.

What are you doing out here?

Ma's talking to someone in the kitchen.

Who is it? I ask.

Some woman with frizzy hair.

What's with the football helmet? I ask.

He says, It's for concentration. Distracting forces see it and it renders them useless.

I have no idea what he just said.

I say, Where'd you get it?

I found it in the basement, he says. I would hypothesize that it belonged to our dad.

Oh, I say.

The chin strap makes his face look smashed.

It's a day for interesting headgear, he says, pointing to my hardhat.

I found it, I say.

He doesn't ask where.

I don't think he's at all interested in my life.

Sometimes I feel like I'm his little brother and I should be following him around.

We are quiet and he types for a minute.

Did you see the rainbow? Cheedle asks.

No, I say, I missed it.

It was strange, he says, still typing. The rain was coming down in a veritable deluge and then it suddenly stopped and there was a full rainbow.

Huh, I say. What's a reversible luge?

*Ver*itable *del*uge. An authentic downpour.

Oh, I say.

Cheedle says, The Indians believed rainbows meant good things to come.

Then he picks at his ear through a hole in the football helmet.

How's the novel coming? I ask.

I'm having a good session, he says. Glen the Bear Boy is leading me on an interesting journey. As we've learned in

Techniques in Fiction Writing, keeping your protagonist active is perhaps the novelist's greatest challenge.

He stops typing.

By the way, Cheedle says, thanks for the kissing lesson. I told Anna Beth Coles about it today in Chaos and Creativity and she expressed interest in having a lesson as well. She's eleven like you and she's already well into puberty. I think she would benefit from your wisdom on such matters. She said she'd be happy to provide remuneration.

What's renumeration? I ask.

Re*mun*eration, he says. A fee for your services.

Oh, I say.

I think about getting a fee for my services and it strikes me that this would be a form of prostitution.

Eric Duggan told me that prostitutes don't wear any underwear and make a thousand dollars an hour. He got this information from a late-night HBO special.

What did you think of *Anna Karenina?* Cheedle asks.

I couldn't read it, I say. I kept getting stuck on the names.

He says, Tolstoy takes some getting used to.

He adjusts the chin strap and cleans his thumbnail.

Anna Karenina winds up jumping in front of a train, he adds. One of the most tragic moments in Russian literature.

Why does she do that? I say.

I don't know, Cheedle says. I guess she'd had enough.

I see myself jumping in front of one of the Metra Rock Island trains. I can hear the whistle screaming as it pulls into

Union Station. But instead of jumping I get scared and sit down on the platform.

I say, The Sherpas believed that the Indominable Snowman was a time traveler.

Cheedle watches me for a moment and says, It's *abominable*.

Oh, I say. Isn't that what I said?

You said *indominable*. Indominable's not a word. But that's a valuable piece of information. Thank you.

You're welcome, I say, and I just stay there. I put my hand on the swing set. The rust feels cold and prickly.

Do you think he has anything to do with the Smudge Man? I ask.

Cheedle says, Perhaps, and starts typing again.

When I walk into the house Ma and the Ham Lady are talking to each other at the kitchen table.

When they see me nobody says anything for a moment.

You can hear the lights humming over the table.

After a minute Ma says, Why are you so wet, Blacky? Didn't you get the bus home?

I missed it, I say.

You missed it.

Bathroom emergency.

Oh, she says. Well, walking is good exercise.

I look out the window toward the woods. Someone has spray-painted FUCK on the dead Ford Taurus.

Ma fidgets a little and says, Do you remember Ms. Wolf, Blacky?

The Ham Lady says, Hello, Blacky.

Hello, I say.

Ma is so tired she can hardly keep her body up. Her hair is stringy and matted. It stops looking red when it gets like that. I almost want to put a napkin over it.

Busy day at school? the Ham Lady asks.

Yes, I say. Pretty busy.

How are your feet doing? she asks.

Better, I say.

They're stinging even as I'm standing there.

The Ham Lady is playing with that blue squeeze ball again. I imagine that she takes this item everywhere. I see her fiddling with it on a plane. I see her on a horse with it, too. The horse bucks her into a lake with sharks and piranhas but she hangs on to the ball.

I want them to ask me about my hardhat but they won't. I'm holding it out in front of me and trying to be obvious.

Ma looks at the Ham Lady with a very pained expression on her face. For a second it gets so quiet you can hear the refrigerator and the lights humming. It's like they're doing a duet.

Ma says, Did you get your makeup assignments?

Yes, I say.

She's doing this thing where she's not looking at me. It's like she's been replaced by a machine person. If I opened her up I'd probably find vacuum cleaner parts.

The Ham Lady turns to me and then she glances at Ma and smiles. Her teeth seem too small for her mouth.

Is Shay home? I ask.

She's in her room, Ma says.

Okay, I say.

We'll just be a few more minutes, Blacky, the Ham Lady says, still smiling.

Go dry your head, Ma says, but she's still not looking at me.

She's making a guess.

She's looking at the toaster like it's going to say something back.

I put my hardhat under my bed and go into Shay's room.

Shay is listening to music that sounds like cars on a speedway.

Her headphones make her look like she's part UFO. Her hair is so red you can close your eyes and still see it.

The thing about Shay is that she disappears a lot.

It's like living with an escape artist.

She sneaks in and out of her window like a jewel thief. If you look behind her blue curtains you can see how the screen's bent. You can also see many cigarette butts.

A lot of her clothes are ripped cause of all the criminal activity. Once I saw her nipple poking through a hole in her shirt.

Sometimes Ma pleads with Shay to wear a bra. She'll say, C'mon, Shay, wear a bra. What kind of image are you trying to project?

Shay's seventeen and last year she had a baby that came out dead. She got sick shortly after this and it was discovered that she had hepatitis.

Ma borrowed some money from her brother Jack and sent Shay to this place in Michigan called Open Grove Recovery Facility. Shay said it was full of rich kids who were junkies and prostitutes.

When we drove up to visit her there was a snowstorm and the maple trees were so white Ma said she was going to write a poem about them, but she never did.

We got to sit in this room with Shay and there was a foosball table and I played against an African American boy with a burnt face while Shay and Ma sat in chairs and stared at each other.

The boy with the burnt face beat me twelve games in a row. Some of his face was brown but most of it was pink and rubbery-looking. I think I had a hard time concentrating cause of this fact.

After he beat me twelve times he played with one hand and beat me twice more.

He was an excellent foosball player. I imagine he could be a professional.

When we said goodbye Shay cried so hard snots came out of her nose.

She kept saying she was going to get clean.

I'm gonna get clean, Ma, I promise, she said. I promise I'll get clean, please let me come home!

She begged like an animal but Ma made her stay at Open Grove Recovery Facility and cried the whole drive back.

Shay stayed there for a month and when she finally came home she seemed sad and fragile.

One night I asked her about the dead baby.

She said that she dreams about it sometimes and its name is Bruce.

Her boyfriend at the time didn't even know about Bruce the Dead Baby. His name is Dennis Parker and he's in the Marines now.

Ma thought that after being at Open Grove Shay would change her ways but she hasn't.

Ma says, What are we gonna do with Shay?

Ma says, I wasted all my brother's money.

Now Shay's got more than one boyfriend.

I saw this guy in her room with her once. His name is Speed and he's got a tattoo of a dragon on his back. He's so pale the first time I saw him I thought he was a vampire.

Over the summer Shay had a job at Sizzler but she got caught smoking marijuana in the employee bathroom. Now she doesn't work and it creates a lot of tension between her and Ma.

Hey, I say, but she doesn't hear me. Her room smells like cigarettes and air freshener.

I come up over her shoulder. Her hands are shaking so bad it's like they're someone else's hands.

I poke her in the back.

Shay turns and takes her headphones off.

A woman is singing to the speedway song now. She sounds like she's having a multiple orgasm. Eric Duggan told me about multiple orgasms. He said that women in China have them all the time.

Showtime exclusive, he said. You gotta get that channel, Blacky.

Hey, I say to Shay.

She says, Hey.

I just stand there.

I'm wondering if she can see through me to the other side of her room where her posters are. There's this one of a horse with a human leg and I'm not sure what it's supposed to mean.

What's up? she says.

Nothing, I say.

You okay?

Yes.

There's something about Shay's eyes. Her pupils are so black it's like some aliens took her up in a spaceship and made an exchange.

They used to be a lot bluer.

What are you doing? I ask.

Nothin, she says. Ponderin shit.

What are you pondering?

I don't know, she says. Takin a trip. Movin to Chicago. The usual.

Oh, I say.

Oh, she says, mocking me.

Are you really gonna move to Chicago? I ask.

I'm thinkin about it. Betty says there are these cheap apartments in Logan Square and that her brother would get the lease for us.

I say, Can I go with?

No.

Why not?

Cause you're too young, she says. You gotta finish school.

Then I take out the tongue and show it to her.

What's that? she asks.

It's a tongue, I say.

She grabs it and looks at it.

Weird, she says.

It's from the Dave the See-Through Fake Human. I stole it in Life Science. He's got other parts too. I'm gonna get a kidney next time.

It looks like a dildo, Shay says, and hands it back.

Her comment makes me lose my balance and I do a full circle and wind up facing her again.

What are you gonna do with it? she asks.

Put it in my box, I say.

She looks at me like I said something stupid.

I got this special box that I put stuff in. I keep it in the closet in my room. So far it contains a sweater, a scarf, and a black permanent marker. Later I will try and fit my hardhat in it too, but this will take some special arranging.

Shay's still looking at me like I'm stupid.

What? I say.

Don't be such a freak, she says.

Okay, I say.

You need a haircut.

I do?

Yeah, Blacky. And brush your teeth, you have dickbreath.

Okay.

You know how to check your breath, don't you?

No, I say.

Then she shows me.

She cups her hands in front of her mouth and breathes.

I do it too.

My breath does smell and it makes me feel slow and stupid.

I'll use gum from now on, I promise myself.

Shay lights a cigarette. She smokes Kools cause these are the cigarettes that her friend Betty steals from her mom.

There are three Airwick air fresheners set on Shay's desk. She is always careful to blow the smoke into one of these. One of them is supposed to smell like lemons but it smells more like dirty dishes.

I tried to smoke one of her Kools once but I couldn't get it to go in my lungs. I wound up choking and crying.

The song is over and the next one comes on.

Where were you last night? I ask.

I was in Romeoville, she says. Why?

I say, Cause I came in here and you were gone.

We don't say anything for a second. She just smokes and acts bored.

I say, What were you doing in Romeoville?

She says, Barn party, and leaves it at that.

Are you gonna be here tonight? I ask.

She says, I'm goin to Rockdale with Betty and Flahive.

Flahive is this guy who sells guns and fireworks. Roman candles are five bucks.

Five bucks for a Roman candle, he'll say to me sometimes. You got five bucks?

He's much older than most of the kids he hangs out with. He wears an army jacket and drives a Kawasaki motorcycle. It's black with lots of red trim. The gas tank has FLAHIVE on it. It's written in cursive and I imagine this must have cost lots of money.

He has a tattoo of five tally marks on the side of his neck. Shay says that this is the number of years he spent in Joliet Correctional for dealing cocaine.

Once when I answered the front door he didn't have a shirt on. I looked for other tattoos but there weren't any. When he walked by me he flicked me in the Adam's apple and I barked like a dog.

You're never home anymore, I tell Shay.

Blacky, if you get scared just go into Ma's room.

I can't, I say.

Yes, you can. Just take your blanket and sleep on the floor.

I say, I think she's mad at me.

Oh, everyone's mad at everybody, Shay says. We're all mad.

Cheedle's not mad, I say.

But Cheedle's not normal, she says.

Shay is so pretty it makes me uncomfortable. She tries to hide it by smearing black makeup around her eyes. But I know this is just a disguise.

What's in Rockdale? I ask.

None of your beeswax.

Drugs? I say.

Maybe.

I say, You're gonna get hepatitis again.

She says, No, I ain't.

Ma will put you back in Open Grove.

No, she won't, Shay says. We don't even have the money.

Shay is wearing this sweatsuit that she stole from the mall. It's dark blue with white stripes. When you drag your fingernail on it the material makes this noise like records getting scratched in a rap song.

I say, Can I do some with you sometime?

Some what? she asks.

Drugs.

No way, Creepo.

Why not?

Cause most of the time they suck and besides they're so bad for you.

I say, You do them.

That's cause I'm a burnt-out slut.

I know she is kidding but when she uses the word *slut* it feels like getting punched in the stomach.

Is Ma still talkin to that lady? Shay asks.

Yes, I say.

Do you know if she's workin tonight?

I don't know, I say. I think so. She's still wearing the same thing she had on yesterday. She seems pretty worn out.

Aren't we all, Shay says.

Then she smokes some more and blows into the Airwick lemon air freshener.

I say, If I come in here tonight and you're gone can I sleep in your bed anyways?

Yeah, she says, sure. Just don't piss in it.

Then she gives me a titty twister.

Shay has a particular talent for titty twisters.

I break free and rub my nipple. I get so excited I have to sit down on her lap.

Dork, she says.

We almost smile at the same time but Shay has this thing that she does. She stops her mouth from smiling all the way.

Now get outta here so I can ponder, she says, and pushes me off her lap.

It amazes me how well she can talk with a cigarette in her mouth.

Bye, I say, but Shay hardly ever says bye back to you. She has this weird rule about goodbyes.

Then she puts her headphones on and turns back into a UFO.

In Life Science Mr. Prisby announces that Dave the See-Through Fake Human is missing his tongue.

Dave's tongue is missing, he says. If anyone has information regarding its whereabouts please let me know.

He looks at us all keen and suspicious-like.

He adds, There may be extra credit involved. It's pretty hard to talk to Dave when he doesn't have a tongue, right, Sofia?

Sofia George blushes and says, Yes, Mr. Prisby.

The girls on the left side of the class laugh like it's the most hilarious thing they've heard all year.

Two of them have yellow streaks in their hair and I'm convinced that they planned this.

After the business with Dave we learn about the lungs.

How they absorb oxygen and discharge carbon dioxide.

I imagine myself as a car. I'm parked near the bowling alley and someone has spray-painted FUCK on me.

Mr. Prisby uses the overhead projector to show a picture of a lung with cancer. It's so black it looks purple.

The girls on the left side of the room squeal with grossness.

Mr. Prisby says, Not a very pretty sight, huh?

The squealing stops and everything gets real quiet for a minute.

I look at the clock. I have this theory that it moves backwards sometimes.

Mr. Prisby shuts off the projector and says, So don't smoke. It took me nine years to quit.

When he says this he removes his glasses so we can see how serious he is.

Then he puts them on Dave the See-Through Fake Human and gives him a little squeeze on the nose.

All the girls on the left side of the room laugh and this means everything is back to normal.

After class I approach Mr. Prisby's desk.

Hello, Blacky, he says.

Hello, I say.

I realize that his tie is a clip-on. All along I thought it was a regular tie. It's funny the things you find out about people.

What can I do for you? he asks.

I have information, I say.

Oh, he says. What kind of information?

About Dave's tongue, I say.

I see, he says.

We say nothing for a moment.

I find the window. Something blows by. I think it's someone's hat.

I feel hard and dangerous.

Thank you for coming forward, Blacky, Mr. Prisby finally says. What kind of information do you have?

I know where it is, I say.

Oh, he says. Well, that's good. Where is it?

Do I get extra credit?

Well, I'll have to see, Blacky. If you can bring it to me perhaps that could be arranged.

I glance over at Dave the See-Through Fake Human. I keep getting the feeling that he's going to burp.

Eric Duggan took it, I say.

Eric? he says. Are you sure?

Yes, I say. It fell out of his bookbag and I picked it up.

So you'll bring it to me? he asks.

Yes, I say.

Good, he says. I appreciate that, Blacky.

At lunch Mary Jane Paddington is eating a tuna sandwich again.

Hey, I say.

She says, Hey.

She's wearing the same QUACK OFF, MOTHERQUACKER! long-sleeved T-shirt she had on yesterday but it's turned inside out now.

I say, I don't got enough money for lunch but I'd still like to sit with you.

My stomach growls so loud it sounds like laughing.

Mary Jane Paddington says, Here, and gives me half of her sandwich.

Thanks, I say.

I take a bite. It's so good that it becomes impossible to hide the fact that I'm starving.

I eat the whole thing standing up.

Mary Jane Paddington says, Hungry, huh?

Yes, I say.

She says, You don't eat, do you.

I eat, I say.

She says, It doesn't seem like it.

I ate last night.

No wonder you're so skinny.

Right then I think of my body naked. My nipples are pen dots. My ribs look drawn on with a pencil.

Mary Jane Paddington says, You forgot to sit.

I say, What?

A minute ago you said that you forgot your lunch money but that you still wanted to sit with me.

I do, I say.

So sit.

Um. I can't.

Why not?

I say, Cause I think my legs stopped working.

She stands up and says, Do you need me to help you sit?

Yes, please, I say.

She comes over to my side of the table and gently pushes me behind my knees. This is an effective technique and my legs get unstuck.

In the background there are whistles.

Someone yells, skanks! and everyone laughs.

Her hair smells like apples.

It makes me want to taste it.

Here we go, she says, and eases me down.

Thanks, I say.

Mary Jane Paddington says, No problem, and offers her Fritos.

I take too many and some fall on the floor.

In Art I mix paints and continue my Anne Meadows Hair Project. I plan on giving her the painting regardless of the grade.

I picture us on a bike.

We're riding down Black Road and the sky has many colors. The bike is equipped with a banana seat so both of us can fit. Her breasts are pressing into my back and I feel like a lion.

Miss Haze is not like all the other teachers. She prefers to wear old wrinkly clothes that are full of paint. She doesn't give grades based on talent or performance.

It's all about effort in my class, she says.

She never wears makeup and even though her face is young-looking and pretty there are several streaks of gray in her hair.

Eric Duggan says she's a lesbian and that she lives with a fat woman who looks like Mayor Daley of Chicago.

Whenever someone says anything about Miss Haze, Eric Duggan says, Lesbomania.

You could say anything and he'd make this remark.

Once I said, Hey, Eric, Miss Haze is wearing two different shoes today, and Eric Duggan replied, Lesbomania.

Another time I told him how I saw her sneaking a chocolate bar during class and he said it again: Lesbomania.

I looked up *Lesbomania* in Cheedle's dictionary and it isn't a word. The closest thing to it is *Lesbos*, which is a forbidden isle in Greek mythology.

I told Eric Duggan about that and he told me to stop being such a wordsmith.

We are painting to music. It's a piano and this other instrument that sounds like a duck. I have been staring at Anne Meadows' hair for ten minutes. I realize that it looks more like some pants than hair. I haven't even lifted my brush.

My easel is lopsided and I have to fold some notebook paper underneath one of its legs so it won't wobble.

Miss Haze comes up behind me. She sort of slinks when she walks. I would say that her walk is catlike.

Everything okay, Blacky? she asks.

I nod.

Or at least I think I do.

Blacky? she says again.

I say, I'm fine, thanks.

It's okay if you're blocked on this one, she says, almost touching Anne Meadows' hair.

Today she is wearing a blue mechanic's suit with white paint splatters.

I imagine her lesbian lover splattering the white paint on her and this makes me feel like I have bricks instead of hands.

If you want to move on to a new idea, feel free to move on, Miss Haze says. Just paint what comes.

Okay, I say. Okay.

I fold over Anne Meadows' hair and start to paint what comes.

Miss Haze moves to the portable stereo and lowers the music.

Close your eyes, class, she says.

Everyone closes their eyes.

Don't drop your brushes, though, she says.

I peek through my left lid and catch Charles Wilke staring at his easel with his eyes wide open. He is mentally challenged and spends a lot of time in the Special Ed room. Sometimes he picks his nose and wipes the snots on his easel but I don't hold this behavior against him.

What do you see? Miss Haze asks the class. Let the music move your brush. Liberate your innermost thoughts and let go of all those feelings that keep you sad or stuck.

I try and picture liberating my innermost thoughts.

I see a cage with sharks in it.

Miss Haze says, Now open your eyes and complete what you started.

Then she turns the music up and I start to paint again.

My hand moves before I can think.

Good, Moira, good, Miss Haze says.

Well done, Charles.

Excellent, Sonya.

Then she comes over to me again. She tilts her head a little like she's got water in her ear.

She says, You're on to faces, huh?

I just stand there.

That's a nice step.

Thanks, I say.

Who is that, Blacky?

I say, Huh?

That man, she says. That's a man, right?

Uh-huh.

Is it anyone you know?

It's Al, I say.

Who is Al?

Just a friend.

He has a nice face.

Yeah, I say. He's my Big Brother. He takes me to Seiko State Park. We hunt for fossils and stuff.

I don't know why I tell her this. We did that only once and it was pretty boring. We didn't find any fossils and we didn't find anything when he pulled out his metal detector either.

And what's that he's sitting in? she asks.

That? I say.

Yeah, that, she says, almost touching the paint.

I say, It's an electric chair.

Oh. Miss Haze takes her hand back like it might get shocked.

Those right there are the volt things, I explain. And that's where you turn it on.

She looks at it for a minute and tilts her head the other way.

Why is he naked? she asks.

Cause they made him be, I say.

Who made him be, Blacky?

The judge and all the jail people.

I see, she says. I see.

She studies it for a moment and then her head goes straight.

That's a great face, Blacky, she says. Very nice.

After school I don't board the bus again and I walk home.

This time I skip the bulldozer and go into the house that's getting built.

There's sawdust all over the place and you can see where the rain has left stains.

I sit on the floor and play with some nails that are scattered.

My feet are stinging again and it feels good to sit.

The thing about wood is it always smells the way you think it will smell. Nails feel the way you think they will feel, too.

You can see where they're starting to build a staircase. I imagine the upstairs and the bedrooms. For some reason all the rooms are painted blue. Blue walls with gold curtains.

Like the high school colors.

Above the bedrooms there will be an attic for storage and hiding.

I see Ma and Shay and Cheedle and me living in this house. There'd be blue carpeting and wallpaper with gold and black diamonds.

A big white stove in the kitchen.

A TV/VCR in the living room with every cable channel.

A new couch with puffy cushions.

A foosball table in the basement.

I destroy Cheedle in the End of the World Foosball Tournament sponsored by the Coca-Cola Bottling Company and he has to make my bed for the rest of my life.

Suddenly there is a man with an orange hardhat standing on the other side of the house. You can see him through all the wood.

He's got a mustache and he's holding blueprints. His hands look huge and dirty.

I freeze the way animals do.

I stop breathing, too.

I hope this combination will make me invisible.

When he finally turns and sees me I urinate in my pants.

Hey there, he says. He's wearing a white T-shirt and there are stains where his armpits are.

But I am still frozen.

You okay, fella?

Yes, I say.

Talking makes me breathe.

Are you lost or something?

No, I say.

Well, this is a construction site. If you're not a laborer I can't let you stay here. You're not a laborer, are you?

No, I say.

It feels like my head might pop off at the neck again.

I touch my hair to keep this from happening.

You sure you're okay? he asks.

You can touch me, I say.

He says, I can what?

Touch me, I say.

I don't want to touch you, he says.

I say, But you can't marry my ma cause she's not interested.

It just comes out like water in your nose.

He puts his blueprints on the floor and starts to move toward me. He moves with his hands out in front of him like there's a fire.

He walks so slow it's like he's got to tell every muscle to move.

I try to stand but I can't.

I say, Stand. I say it out loud and this makes me do it.

My butt is warm and wet and there's a stain on the floor.

He says, Are you lost or something, little fella?

I won't tell, I say.

He stops.

He looks at me like I'm disappearing.

You won't tell what? he says.

I promise I won't, I say.

He says, Son, I don't think I understand what's going on here.

Then I say, I'm not falling!

I sort of shout it.

I add, I'm not, okay?!

He says, Okay, and takes another step toward me.

His hands look too big for his body. Like they might fall off and start crawling around on the floor.

Do you need some kind of help, son? he says.

It almost sounds like he means it.

No, I say, no.

And then I am running.

I don't know how I get out of the house but I do. I just run through all the wood.

It's like my body forgot where it was and then remembered.

I run all the way down Caton Farm Road.

I never look back.

His hardhat was orange and I will dream about this, I know it.

9

When I get home Cheedle is sitting at the kitchen table with his typewriter and staring at a bowl of salt. He looks so clean it makes me want to give him a titty twister, so I do.

He hardly reacts.

He just looks at me like I accidentally stepped on his foot.

I am convinced that he is part rubber.

Hey, I say.

He says, Hey.

I just twisted your titty, I say.

Yes, he says.

That's all he says: Yes.

What are you doing? I ask.

Cheedle says, My fiction mentor said that when he's blocked he sits next to his typewriter and stares at a bowl of salt.

Why?

Employing this technique apparently forces you to find meaning in something that's meaningless.

I think about employment techniques.

I wonder if this is the kind of thing that might help Shay find a job.

I say, So you're blocked?

No, he says. I'm just trying it out. In case I get blocked. It's never too early to start preparing for greatness.

Then he tilts his head and sniffs.

I say, What?

You smell like urine, he says.

I open my mouth to say something but nothing comes out.

So I turn and go lock myself in the bathroom.

I check for testicle hair for several minutes. It's a pointless job, I know this, but you never know when the stuff is going to start sprouting.

Eric Duggan says you get a smell first.

Like in your crotch and armpits.

He says it's something like horses and dandelions. There was a special about puberty on the Learning Channel.

I keep checking for this aroma but I just smell like my clothes.

After I pull my pants up I practice making muscles in the mirror three or four times.

There's not much to see so I go into my room and change my pants.

• • •

Shay's old Betty Crocker Easy-Bake Oven can occasionally get temperamental.

I try to make a Stouffer's chicken pot pie but it doesn't cook all the way through. I stab it with a fork.

I stab it so hard the fork bends.

I come to the conclusion that this was a bad idea and make a Little Tonio bean and cheese burrito and a chocolate cake with icing instead.

I ask Cheedle if he wants any but he is too busy staring at his bowl of salt, so I go into Shay's room.

Hey, I say.

She says, Hey.

Shay is playing with her lighter. She's holding it real close to her eye and flicking. The flame is making her lids twitch.

What are you doing? I ask.

Burning my eyelashes off, she says.

Don't, I say.

Too late, she replies.

Why are you burning em off? I ask.

Cause I'm trying to free my karma, she says.

What's karma?

She says, It's like your psychic load. A collection of all your fuck-ups.

I think of my own collection of fuck-ups. I see myself standing in the middle of a junkyard with rats and car parts.

Your karma hides in your follicles, Shay adds. When you remove your hair you free it. It's like starting over.

Will they grow back? I ask.

Eyelashes don't grow back, she says. It's sort of a permanent thing.

In one corner there's a pile of laundry. I can see a pair of underwear with blood smeared in the crotch.

I made some dinner, I say.

You did? she asks, flicking. What did you make?

A burrito and a chocolate cake. I used your Betty Crocker Easy-Bake Oven.

She says, It's a miracle that that fucking thing still works.

I'll serve you dinner in bed, I say.

I'm not in bed.

Then come out to the kitchen.

I'm not hungry, she says, but thanks for thinking of me.

You never eat anymore, I say.

I eat, she says. I just ate something the other day.

What? I say.

I ate a banana.

I saw her eat the banana. It was three days ago and it was diseased with bruises and she ate only half of it.

I say, I love you, Shay, and then I start crying.

I know this makes me seem girlish and stupid but I can't help it.

Shay says, Don't be gay.

Then she gives me a titty twister and hugs me. I squeeze her as tight as I can and then I put my mouth on hers.

It tastes like cigarettes and gum.

She pulls away and laughs.

What? I say.

She says, Don't do that, Blacky, and pushes me.

Why not? I say.

Cause it's weird, Creature Feature Face.

Sometimes Shay calls me Creepo and sometimes she calls me Creature Feature Face. Shay says it's having the combination of pale skin and black hair.

She says, How come you're wearing your Sunday slacks again?

I say, My jeans got wet.

She says, I thought you stopped pissing your pants.

I did, I say. They didn't get wet from piss.

What did they get wet from?

I tell her that I spilled a Coke on them.

Shay looks at me like she knows I am lying.

You can't get anything past Shay.

I used to urinate in my pants quite a lot. It started in the bed and then it happened in other places too.

Once I was in a canoe on Lake Manteno. I was with Al Johnson and he was paddling and I was dragging my hand in the water. The urine just came out of me. It was a good thing I packed my swimming trunks.

Ma took me to the University of Chicago for behavioral hypnosis. The psychologist who tried to cure me was named Dr. Goodwyn. He was short and bald and he had a deep, lazy voice.

In his office there were flickering lights and little things that spun.

I visited him three times. After our last session he smiled and patted me on the back and said, That should do it.

I still urinated in my pants several times after that but I never told Ma. Eventually I grew out of it, though. I think the muscles in my penis grew strong enough to hold it in. I accidentally pooped my Bulls shorts once but that doesn't count. It happened in the parking lot of Dominick's. Ma wasn't too thrilled but she forgave me after Dr. Lamp of St. Joseph's Hospital discovered that I had a gastrointestinal virus.

What did you do with your jeans? Shay asks.

I threw them out, I say.

Are these your only pants?

The only clean ones.

If you give me your dirty ones I'll wash them at Betty's house.

Okay, I say.

She tells me to go get them.

I go into my room and get my three pairs of pants. Two pairs of jeans and a pair of cords. The cords have been in the laundry for so long they look stiff with cement.

I smell them and this is not a pleasant experience.

My room isn't a pleasant experience either. It always looks like someone robbed it.

I take my three pairs of pants into Shay's room and hand them to her.

She puts them in a pile and says, Go eat your dinner.

Okay, I say. But I can't leave cause my legs won't work.

Shay's starting to burn off her other lashes now.

I say, If you move to Chicago can I come visit?

She says, Of course.

Should I take the train or the bus?

Take whatever you want, she says.

For a second I worry that Shay is going to set her whole face on fire. I can almost hear her skin sizzling.

I say, I'll sleep on the floor and do your dishes.

You'll be our little slave, she says, and turns to me. Her eyes look naked and beautiful.

They're bald now, I say.

Shay says, Good.

Then I tell Shay to push me.

Push me, I say.

She says, Why?

I say, Cause I'm stuck.

Then Shay pushes me in the stomach and my legs start working again.

I go out into the kitchen and get dinner.

Cheedle's still staring at his bowl of salt.

Hey, I say, but he's not listening.

He's too busy being a genius.

I wonder if he ever thinks of anything but himself.

I pinch some salt between my fingers and sprinkle it on my burrito.

10

I wake to sleet in the window.

In Language Arts this substitute teacher read us this story about a crow that kept pecking at this little poor boy's window. The little boy was named Jasper and he lived on a farm in Mini-haha, Minnesota, and it snowed a lot. That's about all I can remember from the story. The crow is supposed to be a symbol of darkness and starvation. The story was called "The Boy from Mini-haha."

Sometimes when I wake up I think I might see a crow pecking at my window. If I ever do I will throw Cheedle's big Russian novel at it.

The sleet sounds like a kid crying. I imagine a house burning. There's a little girl inside and she's holding a doll.

Through the window I can see the sleet clinging to the trees. Everything looks perfect and silver.

My room is so cold I can see my breath. It's blue like

cigarette smoke in a car at night.

Cheedle's already gone. His bed is perfectly made and everything's tucked in nice. That big Russian book is on top of his pillow. It looks more like furniture than a book. Like something you'd put a plate on.

Ma usually takes Cheedle to the Joliet Children's School for the Gifted before I wake up. I don't know how she has the energy. I think she wants Cheedle to become a doctor or a famous scientist.

Once she said that Cheedle would start a legacy.

He's going to start a legacy, she told all of us at dinner one night. A legacy of Browns.

She's been taking him to school extra early lately. I think it's cause she doesn't want to run into me, for some reason.

She used to leave notes on the kitchen table for me. Notes that said:

> *Hey, Blacky.*
> > *Have a good day at school. See you later.*
> > *Love, Ma*

Or:

> *Blacky,*
> > *Don't forget to take your vitamins. Good luck on your Math Skills quiz.*
> > *Love, Ma*

I put on my J.C. Penney's jean jacket with twice the stitching and walk into the kitchen for a Pop-Tart. I don't toast them anymore cause I have this problem where I always accidentally burn the corners.

Ma used to make us take two B-complex vitamins every morning. Her dead sister Aunt Diana gave us this huge bottle of them before she died. Last month Ma bought this other kind. It's called Geritol and it's for iron-poor blood. I think they're supposed to be for women only but Ma says it's okay for me to take them too. They're orange and shaped like UFOs. I worry that they'll make me grow breasts and a vagina.

But I have this secret:

I haven't been taking mine for roughly three weeks. Ever since I choked on a sour apple jawbreaker I have a hard time swallowing.

I was at the Jewel with Ma when I started choking. I wandered like I was an astronaut in space for a minute. When I saw her in the laundry soap aisle I moved toward her.

The weird thing is that it was like time stopped. All I could focus on were the lights above the detergent aisle. There were thousands of bugs trapped in them. You could almost hear them screaming to get out.

The other weird thing is that even though I was choking I could whisper.

Ma seemed so far away it was like a movie.

Ma, I whispered, Ma!

She saw my face and dropped some Tide.

A second later the jawbreaker shot out of my mouth and bounced past her down the aisle and rolled into the meat section.

Ma said my face was blue.

Your face was so blue, Ma said. It was bluer than when you were born.

I couldn't talk right for the rest of the day.

Since then I've mastered the Heimlich maneuver. In addition to that poster in the Health Office we were handed pamphlets during CPR training. It's easy if you follow the illustrations.

I practice the Heimlich maneuver nearly every time I go to the bathroom. It works best if you use an object with a point or a snout. Lately I've been using Ma's Head & Shoulders dandruff shampoo. You have to stick it in your abdomen and thrust upwards. Sometimes this action makes me fart but it works pretty good.

I'll concern myself with vitamins and minerals when I grow out of the choking phase.

In the kitchen the window is covered with frost.

It looks like crystal spiderwebs. The field behind the house is frosted, too, and then the woods come out of the field all sudden and black.

The abandoned Ford Taurus looks like it's thinking. The FUCK is still there and now someone has added YOU right next to it. I'm pretty sure Shay was hiding drugs in it for a while.

There was this time I saw her and Flahive crawl out of the

back seat and walk back to the house. You could tell there was something fishy going on by their faces. They both looked scared and excited at the same time.

Once I told Shay that I was going to call the police if she didn't stop doing drugs.

I'll call the cops, I said.

Be my guest, she said. They don't got nothin on me.

Then I said, I hope you get AIDS! and she slapped me so hard I turned a circle. One of her nails scratched a line in my face and it bled.

I hope your foot falls off! I screamed.

Then I ran down the street and hid at the bus stop.

There aren't many hiding places at the bus stop but Shay never came out to find me, so I guess it worked.

I open the kitchen window and look out at the field. A deer is standing next to the car now. It's staring at me like it wants to say something.

Run! I say to it for some reason. Run!

I'm afraid that whoever wrote FUCK and YOU is lurking around somewhere and they might hurt the deer.

Run! I say again.

But it just stands there.

I watch the deer for another minute and close the window.

I try and wash a glass but the sponge is frozen so I just eat my Pop-Tart and hold my mouth under the tap to drink.

The dishes stink like fish and sourness and I know washing them will be left up to Cheedle. He usually does them when he gets home from school.

Cheedle scores huge amounts of points with Ma for this kind of enthusiasm for household chores.

On the kitchen table there is no note from Ma but there is a letter with my name on it. It's in a small white envelope with no return address. I think it might be money from my Uncle Jack.

My birthday's on November seventeenth and my Uncle Jack usually sends ten dollars to be put toward clothes or school items such as books or Mead spiral notebooks.

I think about this for a moment and I realize that I will be twelve.

This is a dozen years.

I'll be like eggs and donuts.

The birthday money is perfect timing, considering that Eric Duggan is no longer paying for my hot lunch.

I put the letter in my pocket and continue getting ready for school.

I open Shay's door and I'm surprised to find that she's in her room for once. When she sleeps she makes a face like her head hurts.

Her room is colder than mine and I find it superhuman that she didn't burrow under her covers in the middle of the night.

I touch her head several times.

Shay brushes my hand away and wakes.

Hey, I say.

She says, Hey.

She pulls her covers over herself and groans.

She says, Why is it so fucking cold in here?

I don't know, I say. The whole house is freezing.

Why are you waking me up, Blacky?

Cause I don't have any clean clothes.

Well, wear dirty ones, she says.

Okay.

Wear your Planet of the Apes shirt.

I wore it yesterday, I say.

What about a sweater?

I don't know where Ma keeps em.

Hang on, she says, and gets out of bed with her sheets wrapped around her.

She digs in her bottom drawer and hands me a black sweatshirt that says BIG DICKS FOR LITTLE CHICKS.

Here, she says. It's the only clean thing I got.

Thanks, I say.

Just wear it inside out. You can tear off the tag if you want.

Okay.

And don't forget to brush your teeth. And scrape your tongue, you have dickbreath again.

Then Shay lights a cigarette and smokes.

Sometimes Shay will brush her teeth with Cheedle's toothbrush. I have caught her doing this several times. Once I saw her using his toothbrush while chewing grape Bubble Yum. I tried to do this too, but it didn't work. All the gum got stuck in the bristles. These are the kinds of things Shay does better than anyone.

I just stand there for a minute.

What? she says.

Do you have my pants? I say.

They're still at Betty's. I'll get em tonight. Just wear your Sunday slacks.

Okay.

Then Shay blows the smoke into one of the Airwick air fresheners and sits on the floor.

In the bathroom I brush my teeth and scrape my tongue.

The water is so cold I can't even wash my hands all the way and they wind up slick and mossy.

I have this one cowlick that I have to wet to make stay down but I decide against it for fear of pneumonia and other cold-weather diseases.

After the bathroom I go into my room and make layers. I use Shay's sweatshirt and my J.C. Penney's jean jacket with twice the stitching.

I wish I had a hat.

It might definitely help matters.

I think about wearing a plastic bag on my head but this would be idiotic and noisy.

But I worry about frostbite.

Once Eric Duggan told me that if you get frostbite various body parts turn black and start falling off. He said he saw it on the Science Network.

I imagine my ears rolling around on the floor.

It is so cold out it doesn't even make any sense.

At the bus stop two kids are wearing snow parkas.

Three kids walk up to the other two. These three are also wearing snow parkas.

Everyone looks like astronauts.

Mary Jane Paddington comes around the corner. She walks like she has extra time for stuff. I admire this and it makes me think of how I always feel slow and speedy at the same time.

I have never seen Mary Jane Paddington on the bus. She is wearing many layers of sweatshirts and sweaters and a windbreaker that says KOREN MOTORS on the back. She is also wearing a blue knit hat that makes her head look huge. Her hair sneaks out at the ears.

Hey, I say.

Hey, she says, and nudges my shoulder.

I try and nudge her back but I miss.

She says, Pretty cold, huh?

Her breath smells like toothpaste and cereal.

All the kids in parkas are watching us like we're on display in a glass case.

You warm enough? she asks.

Sort of, I say, but I know she can see me shivering.

Here, she says, and unsnaps her windbreaker and hands it to me. It's red and says BILL on the front.

Who's Bill? I ask.

My dad, she says. He sells cars at Koren Motors.

Thanks, I say.

We stand there and make silver smoke. The windbreaker helps a little but I can't stop shivering.

This girl with a blue ski vest turns and stares at us for a minute. Her face is pretty and clean.

Mary Jane Paddington says, What are you lookin at, bitch? and then the girl turns away.

When the bus finally comes we get on first and go all the way to the back.

They don't let boys and girls sit together, so Mary Jane Paddington and I sit across the aisle.

Her jacket is warmer on the bus and I am surprised to find that it doesn't smell.

In Math Skills Mr. Stone is walking up and down the rows like a bad-ass. Sometimes I think he wants to headbutt me cause he gets this look in his eye.

Besides being the sixth-grade Math Skills teacher Mr. Stone is also the wrestling coach and he never lets you forget this fact. He's always trying to bring wrestling themes into the classroom.

He'll say, If Ray Larkin, my guy at a hundred and thirty-five pounds, needs to lose eight pounds to make weight but it's Districts and the officials are granting a two-pound leeway, what's the absolute heaviest Ray Larkin can weigh in order to be allowed to wrestle the match?

Or:

If Tom Plano has been my heavyweight and he wants to wrestle for me at one sixty-five and he's been up all night wrapped in plastics trying to sweat off the six pounds he was over at weigh-ins, what's his actual weight before he puts the plastics on, considering it's not Districts and there's only a one-pound leeway?

It can go on this way for weeks.

Once when I was leaving class he said, You could be wrestling peewee for us this year, Brown.

I just stood there like wood.

He added, There's nobody light enough to wrestle that weight. You're a skinny little runt but I'll bet you're wiry.

I thought about wires and imagined breaking a phone and yanking all the guts out.

Mr. Stone said, It's a good way to get the girls after you.

I said, No, thanks.

Then he added, We'll make a man of you yet, Brown.

Today we're simplifying fractions. Eight tenths down to four fifths. Nine twenty-sevenths to one third. Numerators and denominators.

I think this would be a good name for a rock band: the Numerators and Denominators.

While Mr. Stone is at the board simplifying forty-two one-hundred-and-twenty-eighths I take the letter from the kitchen table out of my back pocket and slide it into my Math

Skills spiral notebook.

I use the tip of my pencil to make a slit in the envelope.

I am careful to use very tiny movements.

While at the chalkboard Mr. Stone can get very casual. But if he suspects something going on behind him he'll turn into a secret agent ready to pounce.

All those wrestler types are good when their backs are turned, I'm convinced of this.

After I make the slit I slide my thumb into the hole and carefully open the top of the envelope. Inside there is a short letter printed on a scrap of notebook paper.

> *Dear Girl,*
>> *It's hard being apart. Will you come visit me?*
>>> *Endlessly, Boy*
> *PS. Don't tell your mother I wrote this.*

I wonder if Al Johnson could read my letter from the windshield of that bulldozer.

I wonder if it's possible for people to know your thoughts before you think them.

My face gets so hot it almost stings.

Suddenly the letter is snatched off my desk.

I whirl.

Mr. Stone is holding it over his head.

What have we here? he says. Are you writing notes during class, Mr. Brown?

No, I say.

He says, Perhaps I should share it.

Don't, I say.

Don't? he says, smiling.

His teeth are crooked and loose-looking. One of them is long and sharp and this sometimes makes him resemble a wolf with human skin.

Read it, Chad Orlin says behind me.

Mr. Stone says, I should, shouldn't I, Chad.

Read it, Ellen Hedd says, and laughs.

Please don't, I say.

Through the window you can see the rain freezing.

I believe in lessons, Mr. Stone says to the class. A lesson taught is a lesson learned.

Ellen Hedd suddenly laughs.

I imagine them nude together. He's turning her nipples like dials.

Fuck you, I suddenly say to Mr. Stone.

It barks out of my mouth like a cough.

Excuse me? Mr. Stone says, his face serious all of a sudden.

Nobody says a word. You can hear the sleet hitting cars in the parking lot.

And then I am crying and my face is twitching so much I think it might stick funny.

That, my friend, is a mistake, Mr. Stone says, handing me the letter back.

I put it in my pocket and just sit there.

He adds, That is a very big mistake. I hope you don't have anything planned after school today.

This means I will get an hour of detention.

This is not a good thing.

In the cafeteria I am sitting alone at Mary Jane Paddington's table.

Today's hot lunch menu is chicken patties or veggie burgers. I will pretend it is dog testicles and squirrel feet so as to not get hungry.

When Mary Jane Paddington enters the cafeteria, Andy and Greg Bauer walk up to her and splash her with red paint from a Dixie cup.

They call Andy and Greg Bauer the Crewcut Brothers cause they're twins and they both got blond crewcuts. They have PlayStation 2 and they let everyone in the sixth grade in on this fact.

P-two! they'll say. P-two at the Bauers'! Twenty-four seven, three sixty-five!

One of the other things they'll do is walk up to you and yell, Tornado drill! Get in position!

This usually happens when there are no adults around. Like in the boys' bathroom or near the Science Lab after fourth period.

When they yell this you have to crouch down in proper tornado drill position. If you don't they'll either thump you on the forehead with a knuckle or pull your underwear up your crack. This is called a wedgie and it's not a very pleasant experience.

They can get several kids to do a tornado drill at the same time. Once I saw seven kids drop to the floor.

After he splashes the paint Greg Bauer yells, Skanky titless whore!

Mary Jane Paddington drops her books and then the Crewcut Brothers run out of the cafeteria laughing like witches.

Greg Bauer makes sure to jump over the Paddington Pit.

Andy Bauer forgets to jump but acts like his leg is infested with AIDS and limps away.

The entire cafeteria is pointing and laughing.

The red paint makes it look like Mary Jane Paddington got sprayed with an Uzi. Some of it gets smeared on her books when she picks them up off the floor.

I go to help Mary Jane Paddington but she won't let me. It's funny how she's not even mad.

You don't have to help me, she says.

Oh, I say. Okay.

Then I just stand there.

Get away, she says.

For some reason I feel like sprinting.

I run through the other side of the cafeteria and go to the teachers' lounge.

My body just moves on its own.

I try bursting through the door like they do in the movies.

I use my shoulder and it hurts.

All the tables are empty. The only person in the lounge is an old guy with a push broom.

He's wearing all blue and he's the oldest person I've ever seen.

I am breathing like an animal.

I think I could eat a bug.

Who are you? I ask.

I'm Charlie, he says. The new janitor.

His voice is like a pencil on paper.

Where are all the teachers? I ask.

I don't know, he says. Maybe they went out to eat. They got that new place at the mall. The one with the waterfall.

I picture them all eating chicken wings and soaking their feet in the waterfall. They're laughing and their faces are smeared with barbecue sauce.

I say, If you see them tell them they fucking suck, okay?

He says, Okeydoke, and makes a face like he's lost.

Before my next class I have a bathroom emergency.

I am sitting on the toilet in the last stall.

Above the toilet paper dispenser, in red ink, someone has written the following triple-X smut line:

MARY JANE PADDINGTON SUCKS BIG BLACK DICK.

I imagine her doing this and I have to pinch my arm to stop seeing it.

The door doesn't close right but at least there's a door. The first and second stalls don't even have doors.

Bathroom emergencies are often a product of stress, I am convinced of this.

Language Arts is next and I have to hurry.

My insides feel all torn up and gluey. It's like I swallowed coins and gum.

I almost cry out from the pain in my guts when someone enters.

I can hear feet and clothes and breathing.

He doesn't urinate and he's not washing his hands.

And now there are too many sounds being made for one person. And whispers too.

I can't hold my stomach anymore and my gas farts out like a trumpet.

Then the door to my stall flies open and one of the Crewcut Brothers is standing there. I think it's Greg but sometimes I can't tell.

He is holding a Dixie cup full of red paint.

His shirt is so blue I almost touch it.

Fucking faggot buttfuck sissy! he says, and throws the paint on me.

It's redder on me than it was in the cup.

It oozes down Shay's sweatshirt and gets on my testicles.

When I look up he's gone.

I can hear him laughing with his brother as the bathroom door opens and closes.

In Language Arts I sit still and say nothing.

I think about my collection of fuck-ups and freeing my karma.

I imagine my head bald and icy.

When I came into class Mrs. Brill asked me what happened to my shirt but I had no comment.

Did that happen in Shop? she asked.

I just nodded and took my seat.

Mrs. Brill doesn't push you when she knows you're just being quiet.

She asks Derek Klein to read several paragraphs of a speech written by a famous Native American man called Sitting Bull.

I tune most of it out and imagine that he sits a lot and stares at cows.

I see him wearing a big headdress of feathers and bones.

I see him being a hundred million years old with a face like wet paper.

When Mrs. Brill asks us to write our thoughts in response to what Derek Klein read, I write:

*Sitting Bull sat a lot and stared at cows. He was
a hundred million years old.*

In detention you have to sit completely still. Mrs. Ovitron doesn't even let you do your homework.

She's got big teeth and a face like a kangaroo.

Stillness, she says. Complete stillness.

Roxanne Peterson and Tony Randa are in detention for smoking. They are eighth graders and they always make out behind the high-jump mats in the gymnasium.

They are sitting in front of me and I can smell cigarettes on their clothes.

Blacky, Mrs. Ovitron says, Mr. Stone would like you to write an essay about why it is you feel the need to swear. Five hundred words. You'll place it on my desk at the end of the hour. Is that clear?

Yes, I say.

Mrs. Ovitron says, Get to work then.

I take out my notebook and start the essay.

I write:

> *I feel the need to swear because swearing allows you to use important words that you would not otherwise use. This is not good or acceptable behavior, I realize this fact.*

My hand gets a cramp, so I stop writing. I count the words. It is only thirty-one words.

When I try to come up with other things my head just gets heavy, so I write *fuck* four hundred and sixty-one times and then add:

> *is not acceptable language for the sixth grade.*

This takes me nearly the full hour cause I press my pen in really hard with each *fuck*.

You'd be surprised how difficult it is to write the same word four hundred and sixty-one times while pressing your pen in.

When detention is over my hand feels like it got stepped on.

I turn in my essay and leave.

I look over my shoulder but Mrs. Ovitron is not interested in what I wrote.

She'll probably burn it.

I can practically see her getting ready to light the match.

I walk home on Caton Farm Road.

I don't stop at the construction site but I watch it as I pass by.

There are several men inside the unfinished house. They are measuring things and using tools. One guy has a hammer. It's the biggest hammer I've ever seen. They are all wearing hardhats and blond boots. The guy with the hammer sits and drinks out of a metal thermos. The stuff in the thermos steams up through the whole house.

I get this feeling that if they see me they will chase me down.

So I start to run.

It is sleeting again and my ears feel like vegetables from the freezer.

Mary Jane Paddington's Koren Motors windbreaker is making swishing noises.

According to Coach Corcoran my running form is sub-par.

Sub-par, Brown! he shouted when we were doing the fifty-yard dash. Sub-par form! Sub-par!

After I crossed the finish line Steve Degerald added, You run like a fuckin pansy, Chicken Legs.

When I got home that night I looked up *pansy* in the dictionary. The first definition said that a pansy was a garden plant. The second one said it was an effeminate youth.

Of the two definitions, I prefer to think of myself as a garden plant.

I decide to cut through Hamil Woods. The trees are silver with sleet.

I walk across the baseball field and stop at the Smudge Man's sewage hole. I dip low and put my face near the opening.

It doesn't smell like sewage at all. It smells more like mud and grass.

I wait but I don't hear anything.

I think maybe he's tuning his violin.

Or maybe he's time-traveling to the Himalayan Mountains many centuries ago.

Suddenly a bunch of blackbirds spring from a tree.

When they caw they sound like people screaming.

I almost fall into the hole but I keep my footing.

Here's your chance! I yell down the hole. You don't even need your violin!

I wait for a few more minutes but nothing happens, so I walk away.

At the edge of Hamil Woods I see the deer again.

It comes right out and stands there like it forgot something. You can see its breath smoking out of its nose.

I take two steps toward it and it just stays there.

Hey, I say.

Its fur is wet from the rain.

Its head is huge and solemn.

I take two more steps toward it. Nothing happens, so I take two more.

There's something wrong with one of its ears. Like part of it got chewed off by another animal.

Mr. Prisby will occasionally talk about the food chain and predator-prey relationships. Birds eat worms. Big fish eat little fish.

I imagine a wolf in the woods. It's got yellow eyes and a snarling snout.

When I put my hand on the deer I am surprised at how warm it is. I can feel a pulse in its neck. It's pulsing so hard I can almost hear it.

Up close the deer smells like Hamburger Helper. Its eyes are huge and liquidy.

So brown they could almost put you to sleep.

Then the wind gusts through the trees and the deer jerks away. When it jerks I jerk too and my shoe falls off.

And then, just like that, it's gone.

Like it got thought by the woods and then the woods changed its mind.

I stand there and try to follow its path through the trees but there's nothing.

I leave my shoe and keep walking home.

I smell my hand frequently and I am glad that the deer's still on it.

The houses along Black Road look like they're all keeping secrets. I imagine people staring out at me from cracks in their curtains.

My feet start to sting again and just before I turn onto our street I take my other shoe off and throw it at a car.

It's a green Dodge Dart and it looks very old.

The car is parked, so this is not such a brave thing to do.

But it feels good to throw the shoe and it makes a loud noise when it hits the car.

I almost want to go back and throw it again.

When I finally get home there is a man with tools leaving our house. He is short and has a muscular neck.

He also has a face like a pig's. It's red and swollen-looking.

Who are you? I ask.

I'm the plumber, he says. I came to fix the heat.

Oh, I say.

Tolstoy called.

Who's Tolstoy? I ask.

I think that's your little brother, right?

Sort of, I say. Is it fixed?

Yep. The pilot light of your boiler went out. It's happening all over town. It's pretty common when it gets cold so unexpectedly like this.

There's a black Swiss Army knife attached to his belt. Al Johnson was going to buy me one of these for our one-year anniversary. It was going to be a secret between him and me cause Ma wouldn't have approved.

It's called the Swiss Army Champ Utility System and it's got many functions.

It's got scissors and a saw.

It's got pliers, too.

I imagine taking the plumber's knife and using it for criminal purposes.

He says, You realize you aren't wearing any shoes?

I say, I know.

It's getting awfully cold out to be walking around barefoot.

My hand sort of reaches toward the knife.

You feeling okay? he asks, taking a step back.

I'm not falling, I say.

What? he says.

I say, I said I'm not falling!

Okay, he says.

There is a white van with lettering on one side and he points to it. It says PISTOL PETE'S PLUMBING.

I imagine him in the van. He eats McDonald's and throws all the wrappers in the back seat.

Well, he says, I better get to my next appointment. Take it easy.

Then he walks by me and gets in the van.

I can hear his door shut and the engine start.

Move, I tell my legs.

Move now, I say.

Cheedle is sitting at the kitchen table with a girl. She is wearing a blue plastic raincoat and there is a red umbrella in her lap.

They're eating scrambled eggs with ketchup. It reminds me of this puke puddle that was outside Mr. Prisby's room. No one would claim it.

Mr. Prisby said, Oh, it must be a new kind of mold then, and everyone laughed.

I have to punish myself for looking at the eggs or I'll get sick.

I dig my nail into my thumb every time I feel myself wanting to look.

I focus on the girl instead.

Her hair is curly and brown. It looks more like a wig than hair.

Her eyes are round like buttons. I think they're sort of blue, but that might just be the raincoat playing a trick.

Hey, I say to Cheedle.

He says, Hey.

I notice that he is wearing a collared shirt with a tie. He looks like he works at a funeral home.

He says, This is Anna Beth Coles. She's in my Chaos and Creativity class. I spoke to you about her the other day.

Oh, I say. About what?

Kissing lessons, she says.

Her voice is too deep for her body. There's something fake going on, I am convinced of this.

My eyes find the scrambled eggs and ketchup and I nearly fall to my knees from the grossness but I catch the table with my hands.

What happened to your shirt? Cheedle asks.

Um. I fell on a tomato, I say.

He says, Smells like paint to me.

It was a painted tomato, I say.

Interesting, he says. What about your shoes?

What about them? I say.

Where are they?

I gave them to a blind man, I say.

Well, he says.

That's all he says: Well.

How old are you? I ask Anna Beth Coles.

I'll be eleven next week, she says.

In a flash I see her naked. Her breasts are flat like mine, with pen dots for nipples.

Cheedle says, She's prepared to provide you with remuneration.

Anna Beth Coles puts a ten-dollar bill on the table and says, I feel like I'm entering a phase of my sexual development where I need to explore vast possibilities.

I look at the two of them sitting there. I imagine them singing a duet.

I say, I'm not giving lessons today.

Anna Beth Coles says, Why not?

I say, Just cause.

I feel my face filling with heat.

She says, But I walked all the way over here in the bad weather.

Okay, I say. Give me the money first.

She hands me the ten-dollar bill.

Cheedle says, I would like to observe, if that's okay, and continues eating his eggs.

Anna Beth Coles wipes her face with a napkin and moistens her lips.

Open your mouth, I say.

Anna Beth Coles opens her mouth. Her gums are crowded with teeth.

I say, Not that wide.

The she adjusts her lips and I place my mouth on hers. Her spit tastes like Hershey's chocolate syrup and Twizzlers. We stay that way for several seconds and then I take my mouth off.

She wipes her lips with the napkin.

Cheedle continues eating his eggs.

There, I say. Lesson completed.

Anna Beth Coles looks up at me and says, Glog!

I've never heard anyone say Glog before.

I'll bet it's a cross between God and log.

I'm not sure why Anna Beth Coles would want to mix these two words.

She is staring at me like she might cry.

What? I say.

She says, That's all I get for ten dollars?

I say, One step at a time.

Well, that sucked! she says, and pushes away from the table and walks out.

Cheedle acts like nothing has happened. He just eats his last forkful of scrambled eggs and ketchup.

Sometimes I wonder if he has emotions.

It's the way he just sits there. He's like a rock with a brain.

The rain is starting to get in the house, so I go over and close the front door.

I can see Anna Beth Coles at the end of the block. Her blue raincoat looks bluer far away. I wonder if her eyes do that too.

Her red umbrella is so big I imagine the sky lifting her up and sucking her through the clouds.

When Ma comes home she tries to pretend that she hasn't dyed her hair.

It's supposed to be blond but it looks rusty and dumb.

In the kitchen she puts some things away and then she comes out to the living room and sits next to me on the couch.

I can smell the chemicals in her hair.

It's like the couch burning.

I know this smell cause Shay burned some holes in the cushions with a cigarette once. She was mad cause Ma grounded her for stealing twenty dollars out of her purse.

The whole living room stunk for days.

The burn marks are still there. It looks like the couch got bit by a dog.

Cheedle is typing and watching *Blackbelt Theater*.

What do you think, Cheedle? Ma finally asks.

She is touching her hair like it's changing temperature. Somehow her technician's uniform looks rusty too.

Cheedle says, It looks lovely.

Ma says, What about you, Blacky? What do you think?

I say, No comment.

I think about Cheedle's word: Lovely. Like her hair is a field or a bird.

Ma says, No comment, Blacky?

I say it again. I say, No comment.

Come on, she says. I spent thirty-five dollars on it. Be honest.

I say, What's with your eyebrows?

They look thin and drawn on.

She says, I had them done to match my hair.

You look like a prostitute, I say.

She slaps me so hard I fall off the couch.

The feeling goes out of my face for a second.

When I look up Ma is standing over me like a tree.

There's no need to be cruel, Gerald, she says.

And then she walks down the hall and goes into her room.

She hasn't called me Gerald in so long the word sounds like Spanish coming out.

She slams the door and turns her radio on to a rap station.

What's weird is that Ma never listens to rap.

I look at Cheedle.

He's flicking something off his typewriter keys.

He says, Prostitution is not a profession most mothers find employment with.

I say, What?

But he doesn't bother to explain, so I go in the bathroom and sit on the toilet. I don't have to go. I just sit there.

Later I come out of the bathroom and Flahive is sitting on the couch. His eyes look huge and black.

Hey, I say.

He says, Hey.

Is Shay here? I ask.

Not yet, he says. I was sposed to meet her.

Oh, I say. How'd you get in?

Door was open.

Flahive is playing with this thing called a Zippo lighter.

He can snap his fingers and make a flame. Then he flips his wrist and the top slams shut. It's highly impressive. He does this four times and twirls the Zippo between his fingers.

The thing about Flahive is you don't know if Flahive is his first or last name. I asked Shay once but she just said, His name's Flahive—it's like Cher.

He keeps looking over his shoulder like someone's after him. There are little pink welts on his cheeks. His hair is long and greasy and his nose has a bump in it. For some reason I can't picture him as a baby. He just came out this way.

So what's up? he asks.

Nothin.

How's tricks?

Pretty good, I say.

Whenever Flahive sees me he asks me this and I have no idea what it means.

He says, Stayin outta trouble?

Pretty much.

Then he says, Double trouble, keep him off the bubble, and looks over his shoulder again and sort of sniffs. I can see that his nose is raw and red. Shay's got the same problem and I assume this has something to do with drugs.

We're quiet for a minute and then when I can't take it anymore I say, Can I buy a gun off you?

He says, A *what*?

A gun, I say.

Who told you I sell guns?

No one.

Did Shay tell you that?

No, I say. I just know.

He says, You're a little young for a sidearm, don't you think?

No.

What's your name again? he asks.

Blacky.

You're a little young to be wielding a firearm, don't you think, Blacky?

It's for protection, I say. Burglars and stuff.

I hear that, he says and looks at his watch. It's black with red numbers.

He says, What kinda piece are you lookin for?

I don't know, I say. Somethin small.

How much money you got?

Ten bucks.

He says, It's gonna cost you more than that.

Okay, I say. How much?

A helluva lot more than ten bucks.

Then he stares at me for a second. It's like he's seeing something that he's never seen before.

Come here, he says.

I walk over to him at the couch. He takes my hand and presses it to his chest. I can feel something hard under his army jacket.

Feel that? he says.

I say, Uh-huh.

He keeps my hand there and smiles. One of his teeth is blue.

That's my Glock, he says. It's German. One of the finest makes.

Wow, I say.

Then he lets go of my hand and I just stand there.

You wanna gun, I'll get you a gun, he says. How bout a twenty-two. Think you could handle a twenty-two?

Yes, I say.

Flahive looks over his shoulder and says, Meet me tomorrow behind the 7-Eleven at Five Corners. Cool?

Cool, I say. What time?

He says, Four o'clock. But don't tell your sister I'm doin this.

I won't.

If you do I'll break your pussy finger, he warns.

Okay.

And it'll hurt a lot.

I nod.

We are quiet for a minute and then I say, What's that? and I point to a patch on his army jacket.

Special Forces, he says. Death unto all who touch it.

I almost touch it but I don't. My hand just wants to reach out on its own.

Then Shay comes out of her room. It's obvious that she came in through the window again cause her arm is scraped and bleeding. It's funny how she doesn't even use the front door anymore.

Hey, she says, squeezing her arm with tissue. Her hair is wet and her face looks swollen.

Flahive says, Hey.

Hey, I say. What happened to your arm?

I injured it skydiving. Fuckin parachutes, man. Then she sniffs a few times and says, What's up? to Flahive.

Nothin much, he says. Just talkin to Barry.

Blacky, I say.

Just talkin to Blacky, he says.

Suddenly you can hear Cheedle typing in the basement. He must be using a flashlight cause Ma never changed the bulb.

Shay shakes and Flahive looks over his shoulder.

That's when I decide to go back into the bathroom.

Later Ma leaves.

Cheedle and I are in the living room watching this kung fu video called *The Five Deadly Venoms*.

Ma is dressed fancy and her face is so made up it looks huge.

She's wearing high heels, too, and when she walks it looks like she has an athletic injury.

I'm going out, she says.

Okay, Cheedle says. Enjoy your evening.

I say nothing and just sit there.

On the video this guy is doing toad style on several hundred policemen. They're all using machetes but it's impossible to cut him cause his skin is like steel. His moves look more like dancing than fighting.

Ma says, You make sure you boys eat something. There's bologna and cheese in the fridge.

When Ma leaves she doesn't look at me.

Her perfume smells like flowers and urine.

12

That night the phone rings. We can't call out cause Ma forgot to pay Illinois Bell, so when it rings it's like something huge is about to happen.

Al Johnson helped us pay our bills for a while but now that's impossible.

Even though we can't dial out we can still receive calls, but we don't get too many. Once in a while Ma's brother Uncle Jack will call but that stopped after Shay started using drugs again. Ma's dead sister Aunt Diana used to call, too, but she's dead now.

Once Shay screamed at Ma cause the phone got completely disconnected. We didn't even have a dial tone.

Fucking stupid bitch! Shay yelled.

Ma said, I'm sorry, Shay, I'm sorry.

Then Shay took the keys and hijacked the car. She drove all the way to Griffith, Indiana, before she ran out of gas and got caught by the Highway Patrol of America.

When they brought her back that night she went and hid in her room and wouldn't come out for several hours. Now Shay's not allowed to drive a car till she's twenty-one.

Cheedle answers the phone.

Hello? he says. Brown residence ... One moment, please.

He looks at me and says, It's for you.

I take the phone from Cheedle and walk to the corner of the kitchen where Ma used to hang this picture of Jesus. Jesus was making a miracle gesture and there was a golden halo around his head. Ma took it down after Shay blackened out Jesus' eyes with a Sharpie permanent marker.

Hello? I say into the phone.

Wear it tomorrow, a girl's voice says.

What? I say.

Wear the sweatshirt, she says. And don't wash the paint off.

Who is this?

Mary Jane.

Oh, I say. Hey.

She says, Hey.

On the phone her voice sounds different. Like she's been holding her breath underwater.

In the background you can hear a TV. It sounds like a hundred thousand people are laughing.

She says, Tomorrow I'm wearing my white QUACK OFF, MOTHERQUACKER! long-sleeved T-shirt and I'm leaving the paint on. Wear the sweatshirt.

Okay, I say. I'll wear it.

Then we are breathing for a moment.

I can still smell the deer on my hand.

In the background there's some more laughter as well as a bone-chilling clap of TV thunder.

How'd you get my phone number? I ask.

She says, I just got it.

I imagine her looking through the phonebook and making mysterious calls.

She adds, I already bought some more red paint just in case our marks start to fade.

Good idea, I say.

So I'll see you tomorrow morning, right?

Sure.

At the bus stop.

At the bus stop, I say.

Don't wash the shirt.

I won't.

Then she hangs up.

I hold the phone for a minute and then I put it back on the wall.

In the living room Cheedle is watching the Weather Channel now. It's about the most exciting thing our Basic cable package has to offer.

I want him to ask me who was on the phone but he just stares at the TV.

A woman with huge teeth and a tan is swirling her hands like a witch.

What's going on? I ask.

They're predicting snow, he says. Earliest snowfall in nine years.

On TV they cut to a blizzard in South Dakota.

Get the chains on your tires, it's coming our way! the weather woman warns. High pressure system! Northeasterly winds!

She swirls and swirls.

It's coming our way.

So much snow it looks like nowhere.

Something's going on, Cheedle says. It's not even November.

I am in bed when Ma finally comes home.

I can hear her keys on the kitchen table.

For a second I think I can hear her crying, too, but it might be the pipes. When the heat came back on they started making noises like people having emotional problems.

The toilet flushes and then Ma's door opens and closes.

I count to thirty and then go into her room without knocking.

Hey, I say.

Ma says, Hey.

She's sitting in front of her mirror and making a face like she's listening to music. Her dress looks dumb and rumpled. It's like she's been forced to stay awake for several days.

I say, I touched a deer today.

She says, What's that sposed to mean? and starts brushing her hair.

You can see where it got dyed. How they missed some spots and stuff.

I decide to try and start over, so I say Hey again.

Hey, I say.

She says, What, Blacky?

I say, Sorry I called you a prostitute.

She says, You break my heart when you say things like that.

In Life Science Dave the See-Through Fake Human's heart looks like a bloody fist. Once Mr. Prisby took it out and passed it around the room.

I imagine breaking it in two with a hammer.

Sometimes I don't know what to do with you, Blacky, she says. You and your sister. Sometimes I just don't know...

She's touching her bangs now. She touches them so gently it's like they're someone else's.

Where have you been? I say.

She says, What?

I say, Where were you?

She won't answer. She starts to use the brush again. And she's doing this thing she does when she's guilty of something. She's trying to keep her lower lip from quivering.

Her technician's uniform is bunched on the floor and there's a candy bar in the middle of the bed. It looks like a dog turd.

Her room is starting to get like Shay's.

I say, You went to visit him, didn't you?

She rises off her chair and turns to me.

Yes, Blacky, she says, I did go visit him.

We are standing there like wood.

Through her window I can see leaves blowing. They look like bats circling the house.

I say, Did he notice your hair?

Yes, she says, he did.

I don't respond.

I feel like kicking her closet door but I don't.

She adds, He said it makes me look five years younger.

I imagine her five years younger. She has whiter teeth and a smaller butt.

Are they beating him? I ask.

Of course not, Blacky.

Did they shave his head?

No, she says. But he got a haircut. It looks nice.

Did he ask you to marry him?

No, she says. I would say that that's probably the last thing on his mind.

I say, So how is he?

Ma says, He's sad.

I wish there was a way you could make yourself disappear

and reappear in another room. I've seen this on TV. Cheedle would know more about it than me.

I say, Are they gonna give him capital punishment?

No, she says. Of course not.

Maybe they should, I say.

There are flowers all over her dress. It's the first time I've actually noticed them as flowers. I used to think they were popcorn.

I add, They say when they crank up the electric chair the current makes your eyes explode.

She says, That's terrible, Blacky.

It's all about the volts, I say, and go back to my room.

That night I dream that I am nine feet tall and the world officials don't know where to put me.

There's not enough space, they say.

It's not going to work out, they say.

So someone arrives with a saw and starts to cut my legs off at the knees.

When he looks up I can see that it's Dave the See-Through Fake Human. He's got his tongue back and he's wearing a three-piece suit.

It's cold out there, he says. Gotta keep warm.

When I wake up I give myself the Heimlich maneuver.

I don't go into the bathroom. I just do it in my bed.

I use my fist and bark.

13

Mary Jane Paddington meets me at the bus stop. It is colder than the man on the news said it would be. I am wearing my J.C. Penney's jean jacket with twice the stitching, Shay's sweatshirt, and Mary Jane Paddington's Koren Motors windbreaker.

I am also wearing Shay's electric green ski hat that I found under her dresser and a pair of nursing shoes that I took from Ma's closet. They are soft on the bottoms so I will be able to use them for Gym. Even though they're not Nikes, at least I won't be slipping around. The shoes are so white they look painted.

Shay's ski hat smells like cigarettes and beer.

Hey, I say.

Mary Jane Paddington says, Hey.

Her breath comes out silver.

Janice Caulkoven and Ben Jansen are wearing matching

ski parkas with Thinsulate. His is blue and hers is bluer.

They stare at us like we're illegal aliens.

In Social Studies Miss Cosgrove defined this term for us but I still can't help seeing creatures from outer space.

Space aliens with hard-core laser weapons.

When we board the bus we sit in the back across from each other.

I touched a deer yesterday, I tell her. Walked right up to it and touched it.

Mary Jane Paddington says, Where?

Hamil Woods.

It just let you touch it?

Yes, I say. I felt its neck. Right by the Smudge Man's hole. It was warm and it smelled like Hamburger Helper.

I reach across the aisle and let Mary Jane Paddington smell my hand. I have not washed it on purpose.

After I take my hand back she says, Deer know more than most people do.

I say, You think?

I'd put money on it, she says. My dad used to hunt em. He said if you follow one deep enough into the woods it'll take you to paradise.

I say, Paradise?

Yeah, paradise.

Paradise is like heaven, right?

It is.

I say, Wow.

Mary Jane Paddington says, It's an old Native American belief. Apparently deer hunters try it all the time. But it never works out.

Why not?

Cause it's too tempting to shoot the deer. It happened to my dad, she explains. He was hunting whitetails in Little Chicago.

Where's Little Chicago? I ask.

She says, It's up north in Wisconsin or Minnesota or somewhere.

I say, So what happened?

He followed one for miles. It was a buck. He said it was huge. Maybe the biggest deer he ever saw. He followed it all afternoon and then wound up shooting it right before the sun went down.

Why did he shoot it?

He said he couldn't stop himself. Things got too intense. He got so lost his friends had to call the forest ranger. When they found him he was with the deer. He was hugging it.

I say, Wow, again.

Yeah, she says, Little Chicago was his last hunting trip. He says killing that buck was the biggest mistake of his life.

Mary Jane Paddington turns and stares out the window.

I imagine all those deer in Little Chicago. I wonder where they really get to when they go deep into the woods like that. I see trees and rocks and bugs. Maybe it would be really quiet there? Maybe it never gets cold?

On the way to school the houses get smaller and then turn into the Cresthill Lake Apartment Complex. It's funny how there's no real lake at this apartment complex. There's a pond instead.

Shay spends a lot of time at these apartments. She says there's not a single fish in the pond. She says it's mostly broken bottles and motorcycle parts.

Last summer a high school guidance counselor was murdered there. Her name was Margo Mansfield. It was reported in the *Joliet Herald News* that Margo Mansfield was chopped up into thirty-seven different pieces. They found them scattered all over the pond at the Cresthill Lake Apartment Complex.

The bus driver is playing the radio and some girl is singing about screwing and losing her mind.

In the boys' bathroom I tell the mirror about me and Mary Jane Paddington.

We're a team, I say.

It looks like my heart got pulled through my chest.

My eyes are small and black.

My brown Sunday slacks are looking less and less suited for Sunday.

In the halls you can feel the whispers.

When you look at people they turn away. Even the teachers are doing it.

I saw Mr. Prisby say something to Miss Cosgrove and when I walked by them he stopped saying it.

They're like monkeys in the trees, I think. Like those ones in *The Wizard of Oz*.

It starts with the thumbs-ups.

Hey, skank! Steve Degerald screams in front of the trophy case, and shoots me a thumbs-up.

His head looks bald and hard.

Where's your skanky hoe? Evan Keefler shouts from the water fountain.

It should be illegal to have a voice that deep in the sixth grade.

I run into Mary Jane Paddington between first and second period and tell her about them calling her a skanky hoe.

Just ignore them, Mary Jane Paddington instructs. Let the paint speak for itself, okay?

Oh, I say. Okay.

I didn't know paint could speak, I think.

Silence is our best defense, she says. See you at lunch.

See you, I say.

In Life Science we talk about the five senses.

Mr. Prisby calls the things in our noses old factory lobes.

I imagine earlobes in my sinuses.

Plastic earlobes made in a factory.

Taste is broken up into many centers on the tongue, he

explains. Bitter, sweet, sour, spicy, and others.

In the middle of class he looks at me and says, Any word on Dave's tongue, Blacky?

I get up from my desk and hand it to him.

It's black, he says.

That's the way I found it, I tell him.

The truth is that I colored it with my black permanent marker after that dream I had about getting my legs sawed off. I blackened some other stuff, too. Like two of Cheedle's typewriter keys and page one hundred and forty-seven of *Anna Karenina*. I blackened that entire page. It soaked through to pages one hundred and forty-eight and one hundred and forty-nine, too. For some reason it felt like the right thing to do.

Very well then, Mr. Prisby says, turning the tongue in his hand.

Do I get extra credit? I ask.

He says, We'll talk about that some other time, Blacky. Thank you for returning Dave's tongue.

One of the girls on the left side of the room says skank, but she says it in a private way.

It almost sounds like Thanks.

When I turn around and go back to my chair I can see that it's Anne Meadows.

She has written it in red ink on the top of her box of pencils:

SKANK

In Art I take my black permanent marker and draw dog testicles on Anne Meadows' hair.

Miss Haze watches me at my easel.

Huh, she says, and walks away.

In Gym we do the standing broad jump for the Presidential Physical Fitness Test.

I imagine meeting the President of the United States. His face is wooden and sad.

Hello, Blacky, he says. Did you vote like a good American?

I don't vote, I say, and walk away with a secret smile.

You get three jumps, Coach Corcoran announces. You squat and jump with both feet. Jump as far as you can. You go over the red tape and you're disqualified, you got that, Brown?

Yes, I say.

While we are lining up someone behind me says, Where'd you get the shoes, skank? An old folks' home?

He disguises his voice to sound like an African American.

We don't have any African Americans in the sixth grade, so I would say this is a racist act.

When I turn around many boys are smiling.

Two of them give me a thumbs-ups.

I feel powerless without Shay's sweatshirt.

As I am about to take my first jump, Steve Degerald gooses me and it hurts.

Semper Fi! he calls out.

As a result I only jump two and a half feet.

Coach Corcoran doesn't see the goosing and when he measures my jump he makes a face like I'm pathetic.

He says, Two and a half feet? That's all you can do, Brown?

I got goosed, I say.

You got what?

Goosed, I say.

I'll give you a goose, he says.

For my next two jumps I am disqualified cause my toes go over the red tape.

Behind me someone says, Nice job, skank.

When I turn around Evan Keefler looks proud of himself.

Pretty proud, huh? I say to him.

It just comes out like that.

Go get a shower, Brown, Coach Corcoran says. You might be the first kid in my twenty-five years of teaching who fails Gym.

In the cafeteria Mary Jane Paddington is eating an egg salad sandwich and barbecue potato chips.

We have the whole table to ourselves.

Hey, I say.

She says, Hey. How's it going?

I tell her how I got goosed in Gym.

She says, Who did it?

Steve De-fucking-gerald.

Did you keep the sweatshirt on?

No, I say.

She says, Blacky, you have to keep it on or we lose power. I wore my QUACK OFF, MOTHERQUACKER! long-sleeved T-shirt for the Shuttle Run and Miss Kimsey refused to let me compete until I changed into my Student Handbook–approved gym shirt.

So what did you do?

I went back to my locker and put it on, she says. *Over* QUACK OFF, MOTHERQUACKER!

Oh, I say.

You should've seen Miss Kimsey's face. The Student Handbook doesn't say anything about not wearing clothes under gym clothes.

Good thinking, I say.

There are only so many things they can regulate, she says.

She seems happy and smart.

I feel dumb and slow.

14

I wait for Flahive behind the 7-Eleven at Five Corners. There's a big green dumpster that smells like dirt and vomit. There are also lots of broken glass and a pile of flattened boxes tied with string.

Aside from these items there's not much behind the 7-Eleven at Five Corners.

You get the feeling that an assortment of illegal activities happen back here.

I imagine the Vicelords and the Latin Kings rumbling with murderous urban warfare.

It's windy but I am wearing my J.C. Penney's jean jacket with twice the stitching and Mary Jane Paddington's Koren Motors windbreaker and I've turned the collar up.

On the other side of the big green dumpster there's some woods. I have never seen these woods before. The trees are bare and blacker than trees are supposed to look.

After a while I hear a motorcycle pull into the front of the 7-Eleven.

When Flahive arrives he looks rushed and antsy. He's carrying a small green gym bag that says PROVIDENCE PHYS ED.

Hey, I say.

Come on, he says without looking at me. I don't got all day.

His hair blows around his head like it's trying to escape.

He walks into the woods, so I follow.

About fifty feet in he stops under a tree and looks over each shoulder.

He unzips the gym bag and removes the gun. It's black and nicked in several places. It seems small in his hand.

Twenty-two revolver, he says, handing it to me. Shoot em up Wild West style.

The gun is much bigger in my hand than it was in his. It's so heavy I almost drop it.

He shows me how to unlock the thing that holds the bullets and then he spins it.

It sounds like a ten-speed bike.

He clicks it shut.

I don't got no ammo, he says. Go see my boy Lloyd. He does business in the loading dock behind Costco. A red Camaro with smoked windows. Indiana plates. He sells untraceable twenty-twos for two bucks a pop. Make sure you tell him I sent you or he might go schizoid on you.

Okay.

I imagine what it means to go schizoid on someone. I see an axe and lots of heavy-metal head banging.

So, how much you got? Flahive asks, wiping his nose with the back of the hand holding the gun. His nostrils are pink and raw-looking.

From my pocket I dig out the ten-dollar bill I got for my Anna Beth Coles Kissing Lesson. I also dig out a quarter, six dimes, and several nickels. I put all of it in his other hand.

He makes a fist with the money, then slowly opens his fingers and stares at it like it's a bunch of rat teeth.

That ain't enough, he says sort of sad, putting the gun in the pocket of his army jacket.

I say, But you said—

It ain't enough. I'm a businessman. We're doin business here. I'm gonna need somethin else.

Okay.

He sort of looks over my shoulder a few times. Like there are people hiding in the woods.

You know how to give a blowjob? he asks.

What's that? I say.

You don't know what a fucking blowjob is?

Nuh-uh.

I imagine blowing on Anne Meadows' naked breasts. Her nipples are pink and puffy.

Flahive says, Fuck, and starts going at his nose again.

What about a handjob, he says, you know how to give a handjob?

No, I say.

Don't you ever jerk off?

I don't know how, I say.

Well, he says, this ain't gonna work out then.

He takes the gun out of his pocket, looks at it, and shakes his head.

Then he starts to give me my money back.

I'll do it, I say.

He looks at me and smiles. I've never seen Flahive smile before. One of his bottom teeth is chipped.

He shows me how to move my hand on him.

I think I see a dog running through the trees but it's really a stray kite. I can't imagine who would try to fly a kite in the woods.

The trees smell like dirt and gum. The one Flahive is leaning back on looks like it has fingers instead of branches.

After a minute, Flahive says, You know the Dixie Chicks?

No, I say.

What about Faith No More, you know any Faith No More?

No, I say.

He's having a hard time talking. It's like he's dreaming.

Well, what the fuck songs do you know? he asks.

I say, I know "Row, Row, Row Your Boat," still moving my hand on him.

Well, fuck it, he says. Sing that then.

So I start to sing.

Row, row, row your boat
Gently down the stream,
Merrily, merrily, merrily, merrily,
Life is but a dream.

Row, row, row your boat
Gently down the stream,
Merrily, merrily, merrily, merrily,
Life is but a dream.

After we're finished he cleans himself and gives me the gun.

Wish you knew some fuckin Dixie Chicks, he says, handing me the twenty-two.

Before he leaves he makes me stay in the woods and count to a hundred.

15

At home Shay is packing a suitcase.

Hey, I say.

She says, Hey.

Where's Ma?

Out.

Do you know where?

She was here and now she's not.

You didn't talk to her?

You know, Blacky, we don't really talk anymore. We sorta got in a fight. Cheedle probably knows where the bitch is.

I say, Where's Cheedle?

He was in the living room. But he was talkin about walkin to the library.

Why are you packing? I ask.

Cause I'm leavin.

Are you going to Chicago?

I'm gonna stay with Betty for a while.

Oh, I say. Can you maybe leave her number?

I could but it wouldn't matter. The fucking phone's about to get disconnected altogether.

It's funny how Shay's not packing any clothes. Her suitcase is full of cigarettes and makeup and a bottle of Boone's Farm wine and a hundred-dollar bill.

Where'd you get the money? I ask.

None of your business, she says.

Why not?

Cause it's not, Creepo. I just got it, okay?

Okay.

Then she stops packing and tries to light a cigarette but she can't cause her hands are shaking so bad.

She throws the Kool in the suitcase and starts to cry.

Without eyelashes her tears look wetter than they used to.

I say, What?

Her face gets stuck and she makes a sound like a clarinet. Then it comes out.

She says, I let this guy fuck me in the back of Sub-Diggity.

I say, What guy?

Just some guy from Decatur. He kept following me and Betty around at the mall.

She's crying and she has to sit down.

He was so fucking gross, she says. His hands ...

I imagine a pair of hands. I see these big meaty fingers with warts and sores.

I sit next to Shay on her bed.

Did he use a condom? I ask.

Yeah, she says, he used a condom.

I say, At least you were safe.

We sit there and she cries and puts her head on my shoulder. Through the window the sky is gray like a fish. It seems like it's been gray for so long you wonder if something got clogged up there.

After a minute Shay takes her head back.

Her hands got cuts all over them like she fought off a cat.

I hug Shay and put my head in her armpit. She smells like the bottom of a popcorn box, so I tell her this.

You smell like the bottom of a popcorn box, I say.

Shay says, Don't be such a dork.

I say, I'm not a dork, I'm a skank.

Then she laughs and gives me a titty twister. I squirm away with delight.

Then Shay says, What's that stuff on your jacket, Blacky?

I look down. Flahive's sperm is all over it.

Is that splooge? she says.

It's paint, I say. We're doing snow in Art.

Oh, she says.

I look at us in her mirror. She's somewhere else. You can see it in her eyes. It's like there's this place where she goes that's only for her. For some reason I imagine there's a horse there. The one with the human leg from her poster. The horse with the human leg and green grass and apple trees.

I try to use my brainwaves to make her eyes meet mine in the mirror but the muscles in my mind are not good for that kind of thing yet.

I will learn it someday and then no one will be able to not look.

I think how Shay is so pretty but acts like she doesn't want to be.

There's this kid in the sixth grade who can throw a football farther than anyone. In Gym he can't do anything else right, but he can throw a football with great distance and accuracy. He even throws it better than Steve Degerald and Evan Keefler. His name is Luke Swan and whenever Coach Corcoran tries to talk him into joining the football team he just shakes his head and walks away. I think it's cause he's more interested in fixing cars.

Shay being pretty is like that. Only you have to replace cars with cigarettes and marijuana and other illegal substances.

I say, How old was that man?

Shay says, I don't know. Prolly like fifty somethin. Why?

Just curious.

You got a thing for old men, don't you, Blacky?

No, I say.

Shay says, How old is Al Johnson, anyway?

I say, Fifty something.

So we both got a thing for old men, Shay says, and laughs. It's weird how she knows how to laugh without smiling.

It's the first time Shay has said anything about Al Johnson since I came back from St. Joseph's.

She says, You gotta stay away from perverts, Blacky, okay?

I say, Okay.

Whatever you do, don't get in any vans.

I won't.

And come straight home after school. You're a pervert's wet dream.

I say, What's that?

She says, It just means you're a cutie.

I am?

Totally. You get it from Dad. He was a babe. Just wait. By the time you get to high school you'll have to buy a taser gun just to keep the girls off your back.

I have no idea what a taser gun is. I imagine science fiction weaponry. Something silver that shoots meteor light.

Shay adds, Someday you're gonna be a hunk but right now you're just a cutie.

Shay finally meets me in the mirror and smiles. Her smile is sad and pretty at the same time. She has this tooth that's sort of smaller than the others but it doesn't hurt her looks.

I say, Aren't you gonna pack any clothes?

I'm tired of my clothes, she says, and goes for that cigarette again. This time she lights it. When she exhales she doesn't bother using the Airwick air freshener.

What will you wear? I ask.

I'll borrow clothes from Betty. We're the same size. She's got bigger tits but we're both a two.

I say, Can I have your horse with the human leg poster?

You can have whatever you want, she says. But if you sleep in my bed just don't piss in it.

I won't, I say.

Cause if I sneak home and have to crash here I don't want it to be all groady.

Shay puts a thing of non-drowsy antihistamine pills in the suitcase and closes it.

I say, So what did you and Ma get in a fight about?

She says, I came home and she was rooting through my shit again.

What was she looking for? I ask.

I don't know, she says. But the bitch was all in my laundry and I was like What the fuck are you looking for and she said Don't you dare talk to me like that young lady and then I spit at her and she tried to slap me so I kneed her in the stomach.

I say, You kneed Ma in the stomach?

Yeah, and then she fell down.

Jesus, Shay.

And then she got in the car and left.

Shay smokes for a minute. Her face gets all desperate and twitchy.

I say, Do you know where she went?

She says, Prolly to that lady from Children's Services' house.

I picture Ma at the Ham Lady's house. They're eating sandwiches and drinking Cokes. Dr. Darius is there, too, and he's wearing his rubber gloves.

I say, Where was Cheedle?

He was down in the basement.

Shay looks me over. Her makeup is smeared again. It makes her eyes look like they're fading away.

She says, Blacky, why are you still wearin my sweatshirt?

I say, Cause.

She says, Cause why?

Cause I'm doing this thing, I say.

She says, What thing?

It's just this thing. Me and this girl Mary Jane Paddington are doin it. They threw paint on our shirts and we decided we wouldn't take em off.

I open the windbreaker and my J.C. Penney's jean jacket with twice the stitching and show her the paint.

Shay says, Cool. Who's Mary Jane Paddington?

Just this girl.

Just this girl, huh?

Yes.

Shay says, I detect a note of romance.

I say nothing.

Shay says, Is she your girlfriend?

I say, Um. I don't know. Maybe.

Fuckin A, Blacky.

I can feel my face blushing.

Shay says, Who threw paint on you?

These two brothers, I say.

What two brothers?

Greg and Andy Bauer. They're twins.

Shay says, Fuckin bullies. You should kick em in the balls.

Just then a car horn honks.

Shay says, That's Betty. I gotta skate.

She puts her long black coat on and stands with her suitcase. Her cigarette's still burning in her mouth.

I say, When are you coming home?

Shay says, Maybe never.

Then she fluffs my head.

She looks at her hand and says, You gotta wash your hair,
Blacky.

I say, Okay.

Promise me you'll take showers and stuff.

I promise her.

Then the car honks again.

Shay looks out the window and says, Fuckin weather's
goin crazy. They're saying it's gonna snow tonight. I wish
Betty wasn't such a shitty driver.

Through Shay's window I can see Betty's car. It's big and
green and Betty's in the front seat. She's wearing a black ski
hat and she looks like she's freezing.

I say, I love you, Shay.

I know, Creepo, she says. I love you too.

Then I walk away cause I don't want to watch her leave.

In my room I take out my box and arrange things so the hardhat fits. I have to turn it upside down and put the other stuff inside it.

I count everything cause it seems like this is important.

They do stuff like that in the army.

The front door closes and then Shay is gone.

A second later I can hear Betty's car pulling away.

I'm convinced that there's something wrong with it cause it sounds more like a truck than a car.

I look out the window but I miss it.

All I can see are a few skinny trees.

Later there is a knock on the front door.

I open it and Mary Jane Paddington is standing next to the mailbox. She is holding a can of paint, a newspaper, and a wooden ruler.

Hey, she says.

She's wearing a black plastic poncho.

I say, Hey.

Her head is dark and wet. Behind her the rain is sideways and the wind is blowing so hard the bald tree in Mrs. Bunton's yard looks like a witch's hand casting a spell.

Can I come in? she asks.

Um, I say, sure.

She comes in and takes her shoes off. They're the kind of shoes that they try to make look name-brand. She takes the poncho off, too. I hang it in the closet next to this corduroy coat Uncle Jack sent me that's still way too big.

I close the closet door and then we go and sit at the kitchen table.

Mary Jane Paddington puts the paint and the newspaper and the wooden ruler under her chair and sits there with her hands clasped in her lap.

Cheedle is at the stove stirring a can of Franco-American Beans and Franks in a pan.

When he turns he says, And who might this be?

I say, This is Mary Jane. Mary Jane, this is Cheedle.

Mary Jane Paddington says, Hey.

Cheedle says, Hello, and tears off a few Bounty paper towels with two-ply absorbency for her.

They're extremely absorbent, he says, offering the towels.

She takes them and dabs at her hair and cleans her glasses.

Underneath her chair I can see that her newspaper is the *Joliet Herald News*. On the front page there is a picture of the President. He is shaking somebody's hand and he's smiling so hard it's like he's hiding money.

Cheedle goes back to stirring his beans and franks. His glasses are steamed and this makes him look like a scientist.

Are you here for kissing lessons? Cheedle asks her.

No, she says. Why?

It's just my brother is a fantastic kisser, Cheedle explains. He gives lessons.

She's just here, I tell Cheedle. Stir your beans.

There's an old food stamp stuck to the top of the table. I start to pick at it with my thumb.

Mary Jane Paddington catches me doing it and looks away.

It's been there forever, I say.

She nods and wipes her nose with the back of her hand. The rain makes her hair look black and stringy. The red streaks are more brown than red now.

Cheedle finishes stirring his food and stops the flame on the burner. After he pours the beans and franks into a bowl he grabs a fork and sits down next to his typewriter and eats.

He says, I'd offer you some but there's only enough for one portion, he says to us.

That's okay, Mary Jane Paddington says, and pats her hair with the paper towels.

For a second I think Cheedle is going to feed his typewriter. I imagine it sprouting legs and walking around.

Hello, it says to me in front of the bathroom. Can I borrow five bucks?

While Cheedle eats nobody says anything.

Is that noise from your refrigerator? Mary Jane Paddington asks.

It hums a lot, I say.

It's quite temperamental, Cheedle offers.

Ours is loud too, she says.

The rain goes heavy on the roof for a minute. Sometimes it leaks through the bathroom ceiling. Ma keeps an old Maxwell House coffee can next to the toilet just in case.

After Cheedle finishes eating he sets his dish in the sink and grabs his typewriter.

Goodbye, he says. Very fine meeting you.

Nice to meet you too, Mary Jane Paddington says.

Good luck, Cheedle adds, and heads downstairs.

I have no idea why he says this. It's like he wished us both luck.

After a minute, Mary Jane Paddington says, I like your house.

Thanks, I say.

I see that the clock over the sink is still broken.

Mary Jane Paddington says, I like small houses. You can't get lost in em.

I think about where I'd go to get lost in our house. I'd probably go down to the basement and hide in the dryer.

There's so much rain in the kitchen window it looks like the glass is melting.

Were you born here? Mary Jane Paddington asks.

I was born in the hospital, I say. St. Joseph's.

I was born at St. Joseph's, too, she says. They had to cut me out.

Oh, I say.

I imagine her being cut out. For some reason I see her coming out of a cow. They have to use a saw and there's blood all over the walls.

On the toaster there is a stack of coupons for Velveeta Shells & Cheese. There's another stack for Liquid Drano.

For some reason I walk over and sweep them off with my hand.

The refrigerator hums louder.

The light over the table buzzes.

I say, Wanna go in my room?

Sure, she says.

In my room Mary Jane Paddington spreads the newspaper on the floor while I pick up gross items such as dirty socks and underwear with stains. I put them in the closet next to my special box.

There's a hole in the wall next to the door. No one knows how it got there. I asked Ma what it's from but she said it was there when we moved in. The hole's about the size of a fist and Shay used to hide things in it.

Once I found a plastic bag with blue pills.

What are these? I asked her, holding the bag.

They're my pills, she said.

What kinda pills?

Just pills, okay?

Then she snatched the bag away from me. She stopped hiding stuff in the hole after that.

Now it's just a hole.

I tried putting a poster of Sammy Sosa over the hole for a while. Sammy Sosa was standing in the batter's box at Wrigley Field in Chicago.

Under the picture it said:

SAMMY SOSA AND TRUE VALUE HARDWARE

TRUE CHICAGOLAND POWER!

The poster fell down so many times that Ma made me throw it away.

Our walls just aren't meant for posters, she explained.

Mary Jane Paddington pries open the can of paint with the wooden ruler.

So it's just you and your brother in here? she asks.

Yes, I say. My sister Shay sleeps in the room next to my ma's.

Who gets the top bunk?

Cheedle, I say.

You afraid of heights or something?

A little.

That's understandable, she says, stirring the paint with the ruler. Then she adds, When I was little my dad took me to the top of the Sears Tower. I couldn't get close to the window cause I kept thinking the glass would disappear and I'd get sucked into the sky. Even now if I even think about that window it makes me feel like I got bees in my stomach.

I imagine getting sucked into the sky. I see myself upside down, the Sears Tower shrinking to the size of a bug.

She stops mixing the paint and reaches into her back pocket.

Want some Dentyne Ice? she asks. It's wintergreen.

Sure, I say.

One or two?

Just one.

She pushes a square of gum through the Dentyne Ice foil and hands it to me. She takes one for herself too.

I say, Do I have bad breath or something?

No, she says. It's for just in case.

Just in case what? I ask.

Just in case we kiss later.

Oh, I say. Okay.

For a second I feel like I might urinate but I use the muscles in my penis to keep that from happening.

I say, Can I show you something?

Sure.

I go and get my special box from the closet.

This is my box, I say.

What's in it? she asks.

Just some stuff, I say.

I take everything out of the box. I put the black hardhat on. I put the scarf on, too.

Just as I'm about to put the sweater on, Mary Jane Paddington says, Wait.

I say, What.

Don't put that on, she says. Come here.

I go over to her and kneel on the newspaper.

She uses the ruler to put a blob of red paint on Shay's sweatshirt. She spreads it with great care. It smells highly flammable.

Now do me, she says, and hands me the ruler.

I dip the ruler into the paint and spread a blob on the

front of her inside-out QUACK OFF, MOTHERQUACKER! long-sleeved T-shirt. I am careful not to make the paint blob bigger than it used to be.

I make additional speckles too.

When I am finished I hand her the ruler and she sets it down.

We are so close I can feel the heat of her body.

We stay like that for a moment. The smell of paint is filling the whole room now.

What about you? I ask, adjusting my hardhat.

What about me what? she says.

Do you have any brothers or sisters?

No, she says. It's just me and my dad. And we have a cat. Banjo. Banjo's a Siamese.

What about your mom? I ask.

She died when I was four, Mary Jane Paddington says. She had leukemia.

I say, What's that?

Blood cancer.

Then she takes her glasses off.

Her eyes are odd-shaped and yellow.

Up close you can see that some of her teeth are crooked. One is yellower than the others, too.

We chew our gum for a minute.

My mouth comes alive with wintergreen sensation. I am surprised to find that I have popped a boner.

How's your gum? she asks.

Good, I say. Minty. How's yours?

Pretty good. Wanna trade?

Sure, I say.

I take my gum out and hand it to her.

She gives me hers. It's sticky on my finger and I have to gnaw it off.

We chew and smile.

Through my window the trees are naked and shivering.

Mary Jane Paddington says, No trading back.

Okay.

Is mine good? she asks.

Yes, I say. Is mine?

I think yours is better, she says.

Then her face moves toward mine.

She says, So you give kissing lessons, huh?

I gave one, I say.

I imagine Anna Beth Coles walking home in the rain. Her big red umbrella getting pulled by the wind.

Have you ever kissed anyone? I ask.

I kiss Banjo sometimes but that doesn't count, she says. Sometimes he claws me.

Then our faces move closer and we kiss and all the air goes out of me and I forget how to breathe. It's like I'm a balloon and someone's tied a knot in the pucker part.

This is how time stops, I think.

This is how you make it stop.

Her mouth is moist and warm. It's the best thing I have

tasted in my entire life.

Breathe, she says. Through your nose.

Then I breathe.

I almost like not breathing better.

Then we do it again for several minutes.

I watch Cheedle's General Electric digital alarm clock.

We kiss for a full two minutes.

This must be a new world record, I think.

I breathe a number of times through my nose.

I worry about snots and other fluids.

Later she puts my hand on her breast and my boner starts to hurt.

When it stops raining I walk Mary Jane Paddington to the Rocco Copley Townhouses on Cedarwood Drive. It is only a ten-minute walk and I am happy to discover this fact.

The woods stretch behind the Rocco Copley Townhouses and you can see blackbirds darting over the trees.

We are still chewing our Dentyne Ice.

We are holding hands now, too.

Mine is damp and cold.

Every time a car passes, Mary Jane Paddington squeezes my hand a little tighter. I have no idea why she is doing this but it feels good. After the third car I start to squeeze hers, too.

Even though it's barely four o'clock some of the cars are driving with their lights on. Some of them turn them on when they pass us.

I think this must mean something.

The sky grumbles a little.

A dog barks from someone's backyard. It sounds hungry and mad.

We pass the White Hen Pantry. There's nobody inside except a tall kid behind the counter. He's got long blond hair and several face piercings. There's a little chain that connects at his nostril and his lip. I wonder if this gets caught on stuff when he sleeps.

So have you seen that deer again? Mary Jane Paddington asks.

Not since I touched it, I tell her.

We should follow it sometime, she says. Just to see what would happen.

Okay, I say.

I think those woods go pretty deep, she adds.

Several of the units of the Rocco Copley Townhouses look haunted cause of all the boarded-up windows. This is probably a result of last summer's tornado.

According to Eric Duggan it was the worst tornado in Joliet Township history.

It touched down for sixteen seconds and several houses in the area were permanently damaged. On Rooney Drive there was a garage roof that got ripped off clean. A few seconds later it landed on top of the Hufford Junior High School Memorial Gymnasium.

A kid selling newspapers jogs past us from behind. His

paperboy bag is bulging with the *Joliet Herald News*.

Some people believe that certain gang activities are taking place here, too, such as the dealing of crack cocaine or the selling of Uzis. I heard Shay telling this to her friend Betty on the phone one night. There's supposed to be one entire unit full of Vicelords.

When we get to the main drive I hand her the can of red paint and the wooden ruler.

Mary Jane Paddington says, Maybe next time you can come over to my house.

Okay, I say.

Her hair is totally dry now and the red streaks look red again.

We can do it in the garage, she adds.

Do what? I ask.

She says, Paint each other.

Then we just stand there for a minute.

The sky is like dirty dishwater.

Her poncho crackles in the wind.

Okay then, she says, snapping the top snap of my Koren Motors windbreaker. Stay warm. Bye.

Then she kisses me on the cheek and turns and walks away.

Bye, I say. I love you.

I know she can't hear me cause of the wind but I say it again.

I love you, Mary Jane.

17

When I get to the loading dock behind Costco the rain has started up again.

I flip up the collar of my windbreaker to keep warm.

There are a few trucks backed into the loading docks. One of them says SEALY POSTUREPEDIC and there's a big picture of a mattress.

The red Camaro is parked next to a large van with a mermaid painted on the side. The Camaro has dark windows and an Indiana license plate and a bumper sticker that says TED NUGENT LIVES FOREVER!

I knock on the window and wait.

I get the feeling that someone is watching me from inside the van.

After a minute the Camaro's window comes down and a man with a face like a lizard's looks out at me. I think he must be related to my bus driver.

There's rock music on low. It's a woman moaning to a guitar.

Who the fuck are you? he asks.

I'm Blacky, I say.

Blacky who?

Blacky Brown, I say. Flahive sent me.

He says, *Flahive* sent you?

His voice is like a saw on a log.

I nod.

He sent you?

Yes, I say.

He looks at me for a minute and then opens the door and says, Why you wearin a hardhat, you afraid of gettin hit or somethin?

I'm just wearin it, I say.

Get in.

I get in the Camaro. The passenger seat smells like feet and fireworks.

I say, You're Lloyd, right?

He says, Last time I checked I was.

Then Lloyd lights a cigarette. There are empty packs of Kools all over the floor.

My sister smokes those, I say.

Lloyd says, Tell her to quit. Motherfuckers ruin your life.

After he exhales he says, So what can I do for you, Blacky?

I say, I need bullets.

What kinda bullets?

I pull out my gun and hand it to him.

He studies it for a second and says, This was Basano's. Flahive sold this piece of shit to you?

I nod.

How much did he take off you?

I say, A lot.

He says, Flahive. What a criminal. Fucking thing ain't accurate for shit. You're better off using a bow and arrow. You want me to gas it up for you?

I nod.

Slugs to kill the bugs, he says. Stay here, I'll be right back.

Then he opens his door and looks out.

Fuckin weather's goin apeshit, ain't it?

I don't respond. I just sort of sit there.

Then Lloyd slides out and slams the door.

He taps on the windshield to the van and a moment later the driver's side window goes down and a large African American man's head appears. He's got a gold tooth and a beard.

Lloyd talks to him for a minute and then comes back to the car. He opens the door and leans his head in.

We got a special on bottle rockets right now, you want any bottle rockets?

No, thanks, I say. Just the bullets.

Cool, he says, staring at me for a moment. The cops sent you over here or somethin?

No, I say. Flahive sent me.

You sure?

I'm sure, I say.

I can call him, you know.

I just sit there.

The rain is coming into the Camaro. Some garbage from one of the trucks blows by. At first I think it's a rat but it's only a black plastic bag.

Lloyd closes the door and goes back to the van.

I turn and look into the back seat. Besides several McDonald's bags and a box of Schlitz Malt Liquor beer, there's not much to look at.

The door opens and Lloyd sits in the driver's seat. That'll be twelve bucks, he says.

I go into my pocket and take out three singles and some change I found in Shay's underwear drawer. The change totals eighty-nine cents.

This is all I got, I say.

He takes the three dollars and counts out the eighty-nine cents. Then he opens the gun, removes four bullets, and adjusts the cylinder.

You only got enough for two, he says. I hope you're a good shot.

Then he hands me the gun.

I say, I'll give you a handjob for the other four.

What? he says.

Flahive showed me how, I explain.

He did?

Yes.

Lloyd says, Flahive's a fuckin pervert, and shakes his head.

Then he rolls his window down and shouts, Yo, Barnes! Flahive made this little dude give him a handjob! Fuckin evil bitch!

The African American man just shakes his head behind the window.

After a minute Lloyd looks at my gun and says, You know how to use one of these things?

Sort of, I say.

I loaded your two rounds in the carriage so they'll fire first. Don't mess with it. You just point and shoot. But make sure the safety's off. This is the safety, he says, showing me the little switch on the side.

Like so, he says, and puts the safety back to where it was.

Then he hands me the gun with my two bullets and I put it in the pocket of my windbreaker.

How old are you anyway? he asks.

Eleven, I say. But I'll be twelve in a few weeks.

Don't do anything stupid with that thing, he says.

I won't, I say. It's for protection.

Yeah, he says, we could all use some protection these days. Fuckin gangs movin in everywhere. Motherfuckers are gonna put me outta business.

Lloyd looks out the window for a moment and says, So you wanna smoke a joint or somethin?

I say, No, thanks. I gotta get home.

Then he says, Cool. If you see Flahive tell him he's a punk.

Okay, I say, and then I open the door.

Later, he says.

I close the door and walk away.

The Costco trucks look like they know just about everything.

The rain has gotten colder.

I would say that it is freezing.

As I walk by the van I can feel that African American man watching me behind the window.

I put my hand on my gun.

It feels different now.

18

That night I sleep with my gun under my pillow.

I have a dream that I'm a lion.

I have a mane and I'm walking around on all fours.

At school everyone's afraid of me and when I show up in the cafeteria I roar so loud Steve Degerald's and Evan Keefler's heads pop off.

The Crewcut Brothers' heads pop off too.

Tornado drill! I roar. Get in position!

They all get into position and I flip them over one by one and eat their stomachs.

When I wake up I am disappointed to find that I am no longer a lion.

It's raining again and you can hear it hitting the roof. It sounds like fish simmering in a pan.

Cheedle is sleeping so deep you can hardly hear him breathing.

Ma's with someone in the kitchen.

They are laughing and trying to be quiet about it. His voice is deep and hoarse. I imagine him seven feet tall with a mustache and cowboy boots.

When I go out to the kitchen Ma is serving Folger's instant coffee to a man with a huge back. He doesn't have a mustache but he's got a beard.

I think he might be Native American cause he looks like Sitting Bull.

They don't know I'm there.

When Ma places the coffee in front of him she puts her hand on his shoulder and he looks up at her and puts his hand on top of hers.

His face is yellow and wooden-looking.

Then Ma dips her head toward his and they kiss.

His beard moves like an animal.

In the kitchen light Ma's hair looks yellow and dry. Like Frosted Flakes without the frost.

When they finish kissing the man turns and sees me. His eyes are black and small.

He says, Hi there.

His voice is high like a woman's. He seems younger than Ma.

Hey, Blacky, Ma says. This is a friend of mine. Lake.

Link, the man says.

Ma says, I mean Link. Did we wake you?

I was up, I say.

The alcohol on their breath makes the kitchen smell sweet and disinfected.

Why are you still wearing your Shunday shlacks? Ma asks.

When Ma's drunk some of her *s's* turn into *sh's*.

I say, Cause all my other pants are dirty.

You're sposed to save those for church, Blacky.

We don't go to church, I say.

Then Ma loses her balance and lands on her butt. Link helps her up and puts her on his lap.

Ma giggles and then burps and then laughs some more.

I say, She's not sposed to be drinking cause she takes medicine.

Ma says, Oh, ha. Medicine shmedicine.

Then she laughs and burps again.

What do you do? I ask Link.

I drive a rig, he says. Eighteen wheeler.

Eighteen wheels, Ma says.

She almost falls off his lap but he hugs her around the belly. There's a tattoo of a word across his knuckles. It says LUCK.

Ma says, Vroom, and laughs some more.

Then they kiss and he pinches her butt.

I say, I'm telling Al.

Then I just stand there.

Nobody says anything.

The refrigerator is so loud I think it might break.

Who's Al? Link asks.

Ma says, Just a friend of the family.

Family comes out like *fambly*.

I say, I'm sure he'll be thrilled to know about this, and then I turn and go back to my room.

In bed I try to sleep but I can't stop picturing the Native American man on top of Ma. His body glows huge and yellow.

His beard gets all slick with grossness and he smothers her with his belly.

They hiss at each other when their parts touch.

They look greedy and sad.

Later I can hear Ma crying.

I go into her room.

I don't knock, I just walk in.

She is sitting on the floor with a shoebox. Her face is wet with snots and tears.

I say, Hey.

She says, Hey.

I stand there in my brown Sunday slacks. When I sleep in them they make my legs itch.

What's wrong? I ask.

Ma says, He left.

I say, Why?

She says, Because he got nervous when you mentioned Al.

Sorry, I say.

We don't talk for a minute.

I watch her General Electric digital alarm clock go from 2:05am to 2:06am.

What's in the box? I ask.

Letters, she says.

Letters from who?

Your father, she says. Gerald Senior. He used to write me. Sonuvabitch wasn't a bad writer.

Where is he? I ask.

She says, I don't know where he is, Blacky.

How come?

He never left a return address, she explains. Your Uncle Jack tried to track him down. We thought he might be down in Galveston but we gave up looking after a while.

Where's Galveston? I ask.

It's in Texas. He could be in Mexico, for all I know.

I say, What did he look like?

For some reason I always pictured him as this man that's on a Wrigley's Spearmint Gum commercial.

Ma says, He looks just like you, Blacky.

I say, He does?

You're a spitting image.

Ma wipes her eyes with some Kleenex. Her face is puffy and sore-looking.

For some reason I want to tell her about how I touched that deer, but when I open my mouth I have to close it cause

I think I'm going to vomit.

I walk over to her and try to put my hand on her cheek but she stops me.

Don't, she says.

I take my hand back.

Don't you dare do that.

Okay, I say. I won't.

Then she says, Leave me alone.

So I do.

I turn and go back to bed.

19

Mary Jane Paddington and I are holding hands in the hall. It's just after homeroom and we're at her locker.

Her hand is warm and wet.

Mine is cold and hard.

This fifth grader with bushy eyebrows runs up to me and gives me a thumbs-up.

Skanks die tomorrow! he says, and spits at Mary Jane Paddington.

His spit misses and hits the combination dial on Jenny Carpenter's locker.

When he runs away Mary Jane Paddington says, See what we've started? They can't handle it.

In Speech, Drama, and Journalism Miss Williams assigns impromptu death scenes. We did birth scenes last week.

She says *impromptu* means that you can't think about it.

You just have to stand in front of the class and go off the cuff.

Skip Bush pretends he's at a fancy restaurant eating a plate of fried eggs. Instead of salt the waiter gives him international hitman poison.

He chokes to death and falls to the floor.

This isn't salt! he cries.

Then he vibrates a lot and dies.

Everyone claps and laughs.

Troy Burke takes a hundred million bullets in the gut. He vibrates a lot, too. Then his back hits the chalkboard and he slides down the wall.

When he stands back up he says, Vicelords got me.

Charles Newbill and Tracy Town team up. They perform an old-fashioned Western duel. Tracy Town fires first and Charles Newbill clutches his chest and makes his eyes pop.

He vibrates much less than Skip Bush and Troy Burke.

His knees hit the floor and Tracy Town twirls her imaginary gun and blows on it cause it's so hot.

Miss Williams says, Your turn, Blacky.

I go up in front of the class and just stand there.

Everyone watches me and I watch them.

Someone says Skank under his breath. I think it is Tom Klontz, but I can't tell for sure cause his face is inside his turtleneck sweater.

I puff my chest out a little so they can see the red paint on Shay's sweatshirt.

I feel I am making some kind of statement.

Mary Jane Paddington would be proud of me.

I watch the clock on the opposite wall. The second hand sweeps a full minute.

Miss Williams says, Whenever you're ready, Blacky.

But I just keep standing there.

Everyone is so quiet you can almost hear their hearts shrinking.

Another minute goes by. I don't vibrate and I don't fall to the floor.

Someone else says Skank. He plugs his nose when he says it and Joy Christianson can't help but laugh.

Quiet! Miss Williams orders.

She makes an angry face at the class and they all stop breathing.

What is it, Blacky? Miss Williams asks.

I say, Don't you get it?

No, she says.

I'm a deer, I say. Somebody needs to shoot me.

That'll do, Blacky, Miss Williams says. You can sit down now.

Between first and second period I walk up to Eric Duggan at his locker. He's wearing a new pair of glasses. They are sleek and expensive-looking. The lenses are so clear you can hardly see them.

He shuts his locker and there I am.

Hey, I say.

No one else is in the hall.

It's so quiet it feels like the fire alarm might start blaring.

He says, Hey.

I think I've scared him cause he drops his Math Skills book and won't pick it up.

Maybe it's the look on my face.

What do you want? he says.

I got a gun, I say.

He makes a face.

A twenty-two revolver, I add. It's in my pocket right now. Pretty cool, huh?

He keeps making the face. It's a very disturbed-looking face.

Then I tell him I'm gonna shave my head to free my karma.

I say, If you free your karma then you can start over.

He tries to take a step back but I grab his wrist and we struggle.

Blacky, he says, everyone knows you're a skank and that you and Mary Jane Paddington are having a skank affair.

I think this is brave of him to say, considering I'm the one with the gun.

So I reach around and goose him with my thumb.

I do it as hard as I can.

He lets go of my wrist and squirms away and runs down the hall.

He runs as fast as he can, too.

I know this for a fact cause he is the slowest boy in Gym. He's even slower than me.

In Social Studies Miss Cosgrove hands us our assignments back.

Good work, she says, and passes me Mary Jane Paddington's essay on capital punishment.

It's an A.

When Miss Cosgrove walks away I turn it over and draw my new gun. I draw it bigger than it really is and this excites me.

At the end of class an old lady from the office comes in and hands Miss Cosgrove a note. She reads it and then calls me over.

She says, Dr. Lockwood would like to see you, Blacky.

Dr. Lockwood is the guidance counselor. He's so tall you can't even see the top of his head.

You get called into his office when they think you're going crazy.

Hello, Blacky, Dr. Lockwood says.

Hello, I say.

Please sit.

Dr. Lockwood's office is too small for his body. There is wood paneling and a chair full of stuffed animals. One of the stuffed animals looks like a chicken with a frog's head.

When he stands up to show me what chair to sit in I think

his head will go through the ceiling.

There are two chairs and he chooses the one on the left.

I assume there is a reason for this.

There are things all over his desk. Things to squeeze and spin. Things that hold pens and paperclips. It's so cluttered it makes me think he's got bad hygiene. I see him trapped in a little apartment with dirty underwear thrown everywhere.

When he gets settled in the chair he leans back with his hands clasped on his chest. He's looking at me like he wants to draw me.

I just sit there and stare at the things on his desk. In addition to all of the pens and paperclips there is a grapefruit and an orange. I wonder if they're real or made out of wood.

Blacky, Dr. Lockwood says, I understand that you and Mary Jane Paddington have initiated some kind of clothing strike.

I notice that he has a big nose with lots of dark hair coming out of his nostrils. I try to focus on other parts of his face, but this is difficult cause there is so much of the hair.

He adds, I've been informed by several students and more than a few members of the faculty that you and Mary Jane have been wearing the same shirts for two days in a row and these shirts have splashes of red paint on the front. Is this true?

Yes, I say.

Open your windbreaker, he says.

I unsnap my Koren Motors windbreaker.

Dr. Lockwood stares at Shay's sweatshirt like it's something that should be burned.

So it is true, he says.

Yes, I say.

What does this red paint represent to you? he asks.

Nothing, I say. They splashed us with paint and we decided to keep wearing it.

Who splashed you with paint?

Nobody, I say.

Blacky, he says, you can tell me. Who splashed you with paint?

The Crewcut Brothers.

And who are the Crewcut Brothers?

Greg and Andy Bauer.

He writes some of this down on a pad.

Another pad writer, I think. Maybe he spends time with the Ham Lady.

I see them playing on a seesaw. He is too heavy and has to cheat to make it work.

I say, We're just wearing shirts.

He says, I understand this, Blacky, but you must realize that your wearing these shirts has upset a number of people.

I say, So.

His eyebrows go high and he scribbles something on his pad.

He says, I would say So is not the best response, Blacky.

Then I say it again.

I say, So.

He exhales so you can hear it.

Then he says, I understand that you've been victimized by your peers' silliness, Blacky. But it is unhealthy to respond this way. -

I say, Why?

Well, he says, it only promotes more of the same behavior.

My face gets hot and I have to swallow hard to keep myself from barking.

Dr. Lockwood says, Sometimes we have to learn to rise above things, Blacky. You've heard of the phrase, Turn the other cheek, right?

Yes, I say.

It was something Jesus practiced. You might want to give that some thought. You and Mary Jane both.

I think of turning the other cheek and I see more paint flying at me. All my clothes are soaking wet with red paint.

For some reason I say, Jesus got nails hammered into his hands.

Dr. Lockwood doesn't know how to respond to this. I don't think he had any intention of getting religious on me.

He says, Blacky, does your mother know about your plan to continue wearing this?

No, I say.

How do you think she would feel if she knew you were causing an uproar?

I don't know.

Would she be happy?

No.

Would she be angry?

Maybe.

I think she might, he says.

Dr. Lockwood sits up straighter and starts looking through a file folder. I don't know where this item came from. It's like he was hiding it under the chair.

He says, Blacky, when was the last time you saw your father?

I say, I don't know. When I was little.

He lives in Texas, right?

I don't know, I say. He might.

Dr. Lockwood scratches his ear and says, Does he ever contact you?

No.

I see.

He writes this down and shifts in his chair again.

Have you ever thought about getting in touch with him?

I say, Not really.

Why not?

I just shrug my shoulders. I think it's cause that ache's in my throat again.

Dr. Lockwood just sits there. I notice gray hairs coming out of his ears. This is something I hope never happens to me.

Blacky, he says after a minute, I don't want to keep you too long. I realize you have to get to your next period.

He starts to write me a late slip. His hand is so huge it looks like it would be too heavy to shake.

While he's writing he says, I want to recommend changing your shirt.

But what would I change into? I ask.

Do you have any extra clothes in your locker?

No, I say.

He finishes with the slip and then reaches under his desk and hands me a GO TROJANS! T-shirt. It's white with blue and red letters.

He says, I got a couple of these from the Booster Club dinner the other night. You're a size Small, right?

I nod.

Then why don't you change into this?

He holds it out to me like it's a birthday cake.

I imagine putting it on and never being able to take it off. Either that or the letters would burn into my chest.

I saw Mary Jane at the end of last period and I recommended the same thing to her, Dr. Lockwood says, still offering the T-shirt. The faculty and your peers would appreciate it equally, I'm sure. Do you understand what I'm saying, Blacky?

Yes, I say, still staring at the T-shirt.

I think it will make things much easier for everyone, he adds.

I take the T-shirt.

Up close his hands are death-white and hairy.

He passes me the late slip and I put it in my pocket.

Do you think you can cooperate with this idea, Blacky?

I say, Maybe.

He looks at me all serious and says, Maybe might not be good enough.

I say, I'll think about it.

And then I get up and walk out.

I get the feeling that the frog-headed chicken is watching me as I leave.

When I pass by the garbage can at the end of the hall I drop in the GO TROJANS! T-shirt and keep walking.

In the cafeteria I walk over to Mary Jane Paddington.

She's spreading her food out on the table. Lay's potato chips, a tuna salad sandwich, and a small carton of Nestlé Quik chocolate milk.

I just stand there for a minute.

Hey, I say.

She says, Hey.

Help me sit, I say.

She gets up and helps me sit.

Several sixth graders yell, Skanks!

Aren't you gonna eat? she asks.

I don't know.

If you're broke I'll give you half my sandwich.

I want to tell her what I've spent my Anna Beth Coles

Kissing Lesson money on, but it won't come out.

She looks at me for a long moment and gets this smile on her face.

I say, What?

I wanna kiss you, she says.

I say, Right here?

Yeah, she says. Right here.

I say, In the caf?

In the caf, she says.

I say, Are you sure?

I'm positive, she says, and then she takes her glasses off.

Her eyes are odd and yellow. Even yellower than before.

She leans toward me.

I lean toward her.

The table cuts into my ribs.

We kiss and my stomach feels like there's a balloon in it.

When she pulls away she makes this face like she's got a secret.

What? I say.

I like you a lot, she says. I've never liked anyone a lot before.

Then we kiss again.

This time longer.

When we are finished she scrapes something off my face with her thumbnail.

What was that? I say.

She says, Eyelash.

Then she shows it to me. It looks like a spider leg.

I'm keeping it, she says.

Then she folds it carefully into her napkin and puts it in her pocket.

Do you like me a lot too? she asks.

Yes, I say.

Say it.

I say it. I say, I like you a lot too.

Say it with my name.

Okay.

Do it, she says.

I do it. I say, I like you a lot too, Mary Jane.

Then she says, Say Paddington too.

And I say that too. I say, I like you a lot too, Mary Jane Paddington.

Her eyes get huge.

Just then Bert Underwood, a fifth grader with a lump in his lip, walks up to us. He's so small and skinny it's like he got shrunk at the laundromat.

He says, Greg and Andy Bauer wanted me to tell you two that you're dirty fuckface skanks...

He has to stop.

He takes a piece of paper out of his pocket.

He reads it for a second and says, And that if you're going to make out you should wait till you get back to your slush hole rat's nest called home.

Mary Jane Paddington says, I think you mean *slut hole.*

Bert Underwood says, What?

Slut hole. You said *slush hole*.

He says, Oh. Right.

Then he looks back down at the piece of paper and says one more thing.

He says, And if you don't take those shirts off you're both going to be sorry.

Mary Jane Paddington says, Thanks, Bert.

I say, Yeah, thanks, Bert.

He picks at the lump on his lip and says, You're welcome.

Mary Jane Paddington says, Is your mom picking you up today or are you taking the bus?

He says, I'm taking the bus. Our car's at the mechanic's again.

Okay, Mary Jane Paddington says. See you later in bus lines.

Yeah, see you later, Bert Underwood says. I gotta go.

I say, Bye.

After he leaves we just sit there for a minute.

I say, So what do we do?

Mary Jane Paddington says, We don't have to do anything. Just keep wearing the shirt.

Okay, I say.

I want to tell her about my new gun but it still won't come out.

I'll protect us, I tell Mary Jane Paddington with my mind. Don't worry, I'll protect us.

20

At home Cheedle's on the couch reading a book.

Hey, I say.

He says, Hey.

What are you reading? I ask.

He says, *Webster's New Riverside University Dictionary.*

You're reading the whole thing?

It's a new project. I'm only through the B's. I'd like to complete one letter a week. The word *babirusa* is interesting.

What is it? I ask.

He says, It's a wild pig of the East Indies, the male of which has long, upward-curving tusks. I think this would make a good character name. Babirusa.

I say, Huh, and go into the kitchen to make Velveeta Shells & Cheese.

While I'm boiling water Cheedle says, By the way, when Mother picked me up from school today she asked me what

I thought of you.

I say, She did?

Yes, he says. I told her that as far as individuals go I thought you were interesting but slightly disturbed.

Oh, I say, thanks.

He says, We discussed the possibility of having you spend a few weeks at the Holy Family Home for Troubled Youths. She indicated that she had already spoken to someone in their offices and that there might be an opening as early as next week. I just thought I should let you know.

I can hear Cheedle turning a page.

I imagine his brain getting bigger by the minute. A week from now his head will be as big as a beach ball.

The water boils over and I watch it sizzle on the burner.

When I go into Shay's room there is a fly buzzing on her mirror.

Her laundry is piled higher than ever. It is my guess that she left behind several loads.

I feel like something is shrinking in me.

I wonder if it's Jesus.

I remember a priest talking about how he gets inside you. His name was Father Dolan and it was the subject of his sermon at St. Ray's Cathedral. Ma took us there with Al Johnson a couple of times.

Father Dolan talked like a woman and every time he sang the hymns he made a face like he had to urinate.

Father Dolan said we all have the room inside us for Jesus.

But you have to let him in, he explained.

Like Jesus is standing outside your house looking in the window.

Come in, Jesus, I'd say to him. Can you get our phone turned back on?

I crawl into Shay's bed and stay there.

I wake up in the middle of the night.

It's so late the light in Shay's window is almost purple.

Her covers are bunched around my chest.

My feet are so cold my toes are numb.

I rub them thoroughly and then I get out of Shay's bed and go into my room and climb the ladder to the top bunk.

I watch Cheedle sleep for a minute and then I shake his shoulder.

He wipes his eyes with the backs of his hands and says, What now.

I say, If you follow a deer long enough something amazing happens.

He says, If you follow a what?

A deer, I say. If you follow it through the woods. Something happens. Something amazing.

What happens? he says.

I say, It'll take you to paradise.

Oh, he says.

Do you think it's true? I ask.

I don't know, he says. I might not be the right person to ask.

How come?

Because you're talking about metaphysics. I have a more practical, scientific mindset.

I imagine Cheedle's scientific mindset. I see him with headgear and one of Mr. Prisby's Bunsen burners.

I say, What if I followed a Wisconsin grizzly?

Cheedle says, I don't think you could follow a Wisconsin grizzly.

Why not?

Because it's a predator. It would follow you.

But just pretend speaking, I say. What if I followed it?

Cheedle says, I don't understand what you're asking.

I say, Would it lead me to paradise?

I imagine if you were lucky enough it would take you to its cave.

And then what?

Then perhaps you would become its slave. It would teach you how to pick berries and catch fish. You might even learn the secrets of hibernation.

Does Glen the Bear Boy become a slave?

Cheedle says, I'm still trying to figure that out. He's either going to become the grizzly's slave or his son.

I say, So the grizzly might be a father.

Cheedle says, I suppose so. But that would be the sentimental version, he adds, yawning.

I can see deep into his mouth. His tonsils and throat tissues.

Then he swallows and Cheedle is sleeping again.

I watch him for a moment and then I climb back down the ladder.

I go into the living room and study the woods through the patio doors.

I press my face to the glass.

It's freezing on the other side and I can feel the cold trying to creep into the house.

The sky over the trees is just starting to go a little blue.

Where are you? I say.

Where are you, anyway?

21

In the cafeteria someone has painted the Paddington Pit red.

News of this fact has spread through school so fast it's like there was an announcement in homeroom.

Everyone knows about it by second period.

It's red! Jane Cook tells Mary Lee Broom.

The Paddington Pit is fucking red, yo! Connor Connelly shouts from the drinking fountain.

In Art Charles Wilke is painting with exceptional glee.

There is red paint all over his smock.

What is that? Miss Haze asks Charles Wilke.

It's the Paddington Pit, he replies.

There is mucus clogged in his nose.

Miss Haze says, That's not very nice, Charles.

Some kids laugh.

I imagine him alone in the boys' bathroom. I enter wearing a pair of blond construction boots and my black hardhat.

In his mentally challenged voice, Charles Wilke says, Hey, Blacky.

I say, Hey.

And then I kick him in the testicles and he falls face first in the urinal.

Before Math Skills there is a ruckus by the cafeteria. Several kids are running through the halls to see what it is.

When I get there two men in white uniforms are standing over Mary Jane Paddington. She is sprawled in the Paddington Pit. Her eyes are closed and her body is so relaxed she looks dead.

Underneath her the Paddington Pit is painted bright red. There is bright red paint all over her clothes, too. It's like someone sprayed her with high-octane machine gun fire.

The two men in white uniforms count to three and lift Mary Jane Paddington onto a stretcher.

Mr. Prisby and Principal Jeffries are asking George Lake what happened.

Mr. Prisby says, What happened, George?

She slipped, George Lake says.

Principal Jeffries says, She slipped?

Yeah, she slipped, he says again.

George Lake is a sixth grader with a very skinny neck. According to Coach Corcoran he is even weaker than me.

This was brought to everyone's attention during the pullups phase of the Presidential Physical Fitness Test.

He couldn't even do one pullup.

I did one and a half.

Everyone saw it, George Lake tells Mr. Prisby and Principal Jeffries. She slipped and landed on her butt.

Greg and Andy Bauer are standing off to the side. Greg's forearm is smeared with red paint and he is trying to hide behind his brother.

I walk over to the Paddington Pit and press my hand into the paint.

It comes up wet and red.

After they get Mary Jane Paddington on the stretcher one of the men in white speaks into his walkie-talkie. He says something about her pelvis.

I think it's her pelvis, he says. We're looking at a possible fracture. She banged her head pretty bad, too. She's currently unconscious. Early signs suggest a minor concussion.

When they roll her through the front doors an ambulance yelps like a dog.

Everyone watches them slide her into the back of the ambulance.

Except for Greg and Andy Bauer.

They are staring directly at me.

In Math Skills Mr. Stone is talking about converting fractions into percentages.

Four tenths is forty percent, he says. *Percent* means per one hundred. What's six tenths, Larry?

Larry Gregg says, Sixty percent.

Very good, Larry, he says. You get a doggie snack.

Then Mr. Stone reaches into his pocket and hands Larry Gregg a Tootsie Roll.

Everyone laughs.

What about thirty two-hundredths, Mary?

Mary Berger says, Fifteen percent.

Mr. Stone says, Very good, Mary. You get a doggie snack, too, and hands her a Tootsie Roll.

Then Mr. Stone says, What about eight tenths, Brown?

I say, No comment.

No comment?

I say, I choose not to comment.

He says, Huh, and just stares at me.

It suddenly strikes me that knowing these kinds of things is useless, so I get up from my desk.

Mr. Stone says, Where do you think you're going, Brown?

My brain hurts, I say. I need to see the nurse.

He shakes his head a few times and then I walk out of class.

For the rest of the day I hide with my gun behind the high-jump mats in the gymnasium.

I can hear Coach Corcoran blowing his whistle to start the Shuttle Run.

He yells, Move those sticks, Garner! Move those sticks!

I see Graham Garner's face.

It's red and he's scared.

I think about being physically fit and how my legs feel like dead rubber most of the time.

There is no one around and I just sit with my back against the wall.

I imagine Mary Jane Paddington and her broken pelvis. She's in the hospital and her legs are slung to the ceiling. They got her upside down with her arms spread wide.

But she's still wearing the shirt.

I wish I could talk to her.

The wish gets real strong, so I just start doing it.

Hey, Mary Jane, I say.

She says, Hey.

Don't worry, I say. Everything's gonna be okay, okay?

Thanks, Blacky, she says. I'm not worried.

Then she tells me she's going to kiss me.

I'm going to kiss you, she says. Are you ready?

I say, I'm ready.

So here I come.

Then she dips her face into mine and we are kissing.

Her mouth tastes like wintergreen Dentyne Ice.

It's the best thing I have ever tasted.

I'm really kissing my fist, but this doesn't bother me much.

After a minute I have to stop cause I feel like I am going to vomit.

I think it has something to do with the fact that the high-jump mats smell like body odor.

I think it also has something to do with those cats in New York City.

For some reason I start seeing them falling many stories and splatting.

I see a hundred million cats and a hundred million splats.

I think about how lions are cats.

I see a lion splatting on the streets of New York City.

It has a huge mane and Al Johnson's face.

This is very disturbing so I have to shake the image out of my head.

Then I get tired and just go blank.

A few minutes later I hear my name announced over the loudspeakers:

BLACKY BROWN, PLEASE REPORT TO
THE PRINCIPAL'S OFFICE IMMEDIATELY.

The woman in the office says it twice and it echoes in the gymnasium.

They won't find me here cause it's dark. That's why the eighth graders always come here to make out.

I imagine I could just stay behind the high-jump mats for a long time and it wouldn't make much of a difference.

Every time Coach Corcoran blows his whistle it makes me jerk funny.

A gun can be a friend, I think, so I talk to it.

Hey, I say. Just hang in there, okay?

Okay, it says back to me.

I can hear the lights buzzing on the other side of the bleachers. I imagine all the bugs roasting.

I wait for Steve Degerald and Evan Keefler to come out of the locker room. The passing tone sounds and several boys walk through the gym and out into the hall.

I hear Eric Duggan say something about Beck and his infinite songwriting genius.

Devil's Haircut all the way, he says. Devil's Haircut.

Eventually Steve Degerald and Evan Keefler come out of the locker room. They are always last cause they're so proud of their bodies.

They are strutting gangsta style and singing a rap song about naked bitches and thongs.

Just before they reach the high-jump mats I come out with my gun and force them into the corner.

Whoa, Evan Keefler says.

Steve Degerald says, What the fuck, worm?

They put their hands over their heads like criminals on TV.

I find this so thrilling I almost get a boner.

For a second they are crumpled in the corner.

Baa like a sheep, I order Evan Keefler.

He says, What?

Baa like a sheep, I say.

Then he does it. Baa, he says. Baa.

You too, I order Steve Degerald.

And he does it too. Baa, he says. Baa, baa.

I back away, the gun still on them.

Evan Keefler's nose is bleeding.

And I will never forget this.

After the second passing tone for final period goes off I wait ten minutes and sneak through the halls while everything is quiet.

I see the old janitor taking a drink at the water fountain.

When he looks up he stares at me like I am an animal.

I want to point my gun at him.

I imagine doing it gangsta style with an evil sneer on my face.

He covers his ears like there's a scream in his brain.

But I don't pull it out. Instead I walk backwards through the front doors.

The sky is clogged and swollen.

I cut across the parking lot past the buses.

Not one bus driver looks up.

I walk home on Caton Farm Road.

It starts to rain and the street is shiny and dim at the same time.

It's so cold it's like nobody cares.

Just before I reach the yellow bulldozer, the Crewcut Brothers come out of the unfinished house. They are both wearing black baseball hats and snow parkas.

They walk at a funny angle so they can cut me off with hard-core bully tactics.

They are successful in doing so.

They must practice this kind of thing a lot, I think. It makes me wonder if they have a little brother or sister.

There is a Crewcut Brother on either side of me now.

Hey, skank, Greg Bauer says.

Andy Bauer is standing so close I can see into his nostrils.

His breath smells like sweat and grape gum.

He says, What's up, bitch?

I tell my legs to go.

In my mind I say, Go, legs!

But this is useless and my legs don't go.

What are you doing here? I ask.

We followed you, Greg Bauer says.

Andy Bauer adds, We felt like doin a little faggot huntin.

Then he turns his baseball hat around and puts his forehead on my forehead. This is a trick I have seen used by an eighth grader named Thomas Bazoo. He would put his head above your nose and then snap his neck back and headbutt you between the eyes. He got kicked out of school for it last spring.

Once he headbutted a seventh grader named Cecil Farmer and Cecil Farmer fell and couldn't get back up.

Now Thomas Bazoo goes to a special school for kids with learning disabilities and emotional problems.

Greg Bauer walks circles around me but Andy Bauer

keeps his forehead glued to mine.

I know there will be pain, so I brace myself.

Please let me go, I say.

Andy Bauer says, Tornado position.

I drop to my knees and crouch.

Cover your head, Greg Bauer says.

I cover my head with my hands.

There is a noise in my brain like a dial tone.

Take it off, Greg Bauer says.

He's talking about Shay's sweatshirt, I know this for a fact.

No, I say.

Andy Bauer says, Take that skanky thing off or I'll rip it off!

The rain is sliding across his face and dripping off the end of his nose and into my eyes.

Fuck you, I say.

Just to get the words out I almost have to spit.

Greg Bauer slaps me with the back of his hand.

He yells, Take it off, bitch!

I say, Never!

I squeal it like a pig.

Then Andy Bauer unsnaps my Koren Motors windbreaker and undoes the buttons of my J.C. Penney's jean jacket with twice the stitching. When he gets them both off me he throws them in the mud and bites the neck of Shay's sweatshirt and starts ripping it. When it's all the way torn, they pull my arms behind my back and choke me.

Andy Bauer holds my arms and Greg Bauer chokes me.

I see my face from above.

It's blue like a cartoon.

Greg's eyes are wild. I can see his pupils shrinking.

After a minute they switch positions and Andy chokes me for a while.

I'm choking, I whisper. I'm choking, Ma.

I can feel my head filling with blood. I can also feel my heart crawling up my throat like a snail.

After they're done choking me Andy Bauer looks around for a second and says, Let's piss on him.

His breath is hot and snotty.

Greg Bauer says, Yeah, let's piss on the skank.

Then Greg Bauer undoes his pants and takes his penis out.

It is small and white and rubbery-looking.

He wiggles it for a second and then urinates on my chest. His urine is warm and smells like Ajax floor cleaner.

It steams up into my face and I cough and puke air.

When he is finished they pull off Ma's nursing shoes and my brown Sunday slacks and fling them.

After a minute they let go and I cough and spit.

They are laughing and calling me a bitch.

Bitch! Andy Bauer says.

Bitch-ass ho! Greg Bauer adds.

I get one of my arms free and go for my windbreaker.

I move slow and careful.

When I pull out my gun they jump back and fling their arms in the air.

I make sure to move the safety to the OFF position.

Where'd you get that? Greg Bauer asks.

I just got it, I say.

My arms are shaking and so are my legs but I stand and point the gun at them.

Stand back to back, I order them.

I keep the gun pointed at Greg Bauer's head.

Okay, he says. Okay, okay.

They stand back to back.

Greg Bauer is facing me now and his cheeks are wet with tears.

Jesus, Blacky, Andy Bauer says. Jesus.

He starts to cry, too.

Jesus fuckin A, man, Greg Bauer says. His voice is suddenly high and girlish.

When I fire, the noise is so loud it makes my ears ring. Some birds spring from the roof of another half-made house behind me.

I am disappointed to discover that I have missed.

Then Greg and Andy Bauer turn and start running wild. Greg Bauer falls and Andy Bauer has to help him up. There's mud smeared in his crewcut.

I fire again and hit the windshield of the yellow bulldozer. The glass turns into a spiderweb. The noise makes me slip and fall.

Greg and Andy Bauer run through the unfinished house and disappear.

After a minute I realize that I am in mud.

I'm wearing my underwear and socks and nothing else.

I've blown my only two bullets.

I wonder where all the men with the hardhats are.

My socks are black with holes and I can see my toes.

Wiggle, I tell them, but they won't move.

I realize that I haven't changed my socks in several days.

And I haven't taken a shower since that time in Gym after dodgeball.

The rain is cold and the cuts in my feet still sting.

I stay in the mud for a while and watch the sky. It's so gray it's almost brown.

Get up, I tell my body.

But I just lie there.

A few minutes later I try it again. I yell, Get up!

But it's no use.

I'm not falling! I yell at the house.

I yell it at the yellow bulldozer, too. I'm not falling! I yell.

After a while I finally stand and go get Ma's shoes and my brown Sunday slacks. They're sopping wet and muddy.

It takes a minute but I manage to get dressed and walk home in the rain.

22

From the street our house looks like it would disappear in the snow.

Maybe it's cause it doesn't really have a color.

It used to have a color, though, I think. It was blue just the other day...

I crawl in through Shay's window.

The screen scrapes my arm and I bleed.

When I walk down the hall I feel like I'm floating.

On the kitchen table there is a brochure from the Holy Family Home for Troubled Youths.

I open it up.

Inside there are a bunch of kids smiling. Most of them are African American or Latino.

One of them is talking to a priest.

Another one is making something with yarn and popsicle sticks.

Everyone looks clean and friendly.

I close the brochure and leave it on the table.

In the bathroom I take the clippers out of the medicine chest and shave my head. I can't get all the hair off but I get pretty close.

My black hair is piled in the sink. It is wet and gross-looking. I try to scoop it into the garbage but a lot of it sticks to the red paint on my palm.

In the mirror my skull looks strange.

I am ugly and there's no escaping this fact.

I am an egg, I think.

I am more egg than human.

After I put the clippers back in the medicine chest I go into Shay's room and burrow under the covers.

My head feels cold and hard.

Later I can hear Ma and Cheedle in the kitchen. They're trying to keep their voices low like they got big plans for stuff.

Is he home? Ma asks.

Cheedle says, I think he's in Shay's room.

Would you go get him, please? I'd like to get this whole Holy Family thing over with. Father Harold said we could register tomorrow.

I throw the covers off and quickly crawl under the bed.

I turn on my side so I can spy.

When Cheedle comes in the room he stands in front of

Shay's mirror for a minute.

He's wearing a suit and tie.

He looks clean and impressive.

His hair is combed to perfection.

He takes Shay's lemon Airwick air freshener and smells it. When he sets it down he looks at his hand and rubs his fingers together. Then he touches his hair and turns and leaves.

He's not in there, I hear him tell Ma in the kitchen.

Well, Ma says, we have to tell him.

Later the TV goes on. It's *Blackbelt Theater* and there's lots of clanging.

That night I can't sleep.

I watch Shay's window for a while and smell my body.

I rub my new head, too.

I go out to the kitchen and try to call Mary Jane Paddington at the hospital. Ma keeps the number to St. Joseph's written on a piece of tape over the phone.

I dial the number but a robot woman from the phone company comes on the line and says something about calling the Illinois Bell billing center.

I say, It's okay, Mary Jane. Everything's gonna be okay, okay?

Then I put the phone back on the wall and just stand there in the kitchen.

The refrigerator hums.

The clock is still stuck on six-thirty.

After a while I go into my room.

I climb the bunk bed ladder and watch Cheedle. He is sleeping so hard it looks like it hurts.

I poke him in the shoulder and he stirs.

Hey, I say. Cheedle.

He says, Hey, but doesn't open his eyes.

Look at me, I say.

Cheedle looks.

I want him to notice my new head but he just makes a face like he's confused.

Mother needs to speak with you, he says after a minute. It's quite an urgent matter.

I look at him for a minute and then I say, What happens to Glen the Bear Boy?

He says, What?

The boy from your novel, I say. What happens to him?

Cheedle says, He learns how to hibernate.

Oh, I say. How long do bears hibernate for?

For several months at a time, he says. Often for an entire winter.

Oh, I say. What about deer?

He says, Deer don't hibernate.

I say, They just live in the snow?

He says, I think they do a lot of huddling.

What about humans? I say.

What about them?

Can they hibernate too?

He says, Not that I'm aware of. But I would venture to say that a human raised by a Wisconsin grizzly might learn how.

I say, You don't know as much as they say you do.

Cheedle watches me for a moment and then, just like that, he is sleeping again. It's like he has a switch.

I am tempted to plug his nose but I don't.

I let myself down and get my box and put on the sweater. It's dark blue with a red stripe. I also wrap the scarf around my neck and put the hardhat on for protection. Over the sweater I layer with my J.C. Penney's jean jacket with twice the stitching and Mary Jane Paddington's Koren Motors windbreaker.

I put my hand on Ma's door for a second but the fake wood feels funny, so I leave.

I crawl back through Shay's window.

I hardly make a noise.

In the poplar tree there is a frozen cat. It's the same gray one with white stripes. Its two front paws are raised over its head and it looks like it's flying. The strange thing is that one eye is closed and one is open.

Like it's winking at me.

Like it's saying Ha.

Ma has left the Wiffle ball bat underneath the swing set. The rug from the bathroom is heaped on the ground. When I touch it it's stiff with frost.

I take the Wiffle ball bat and knock the cat out of the tree.

When it falls it crunches.

It looks smaller on the ground than it did in the tree.

I try to close the open eye but it won't budge. There's an ant frozen on its pupil.

For some reason I start talking to the cat.

I say, Hey, but it doesn't respond.

I say, What's nine twenty-sevenths?

After it doesn't answer I fling it into Mrs. Bunton's yard. When it lands it sticks in a position like it's trying to swim.

I go to Ma's window and watch her in her bed.

Ma, I say, but she can't hear me cause she's sleeping. She's wearing her green technician's uniform and her eczema creams are resting on her stomach.

Her hair looks like hay.

I say it again.

I say, Ma.

When she doesn't stir I wave to her and walk away from the window.

The grass is frozen gray.

The sky is so black I think it might start bleeding.

The moon looks like an ice ball.

In the field the Ford Taurus is browner than I remembered. Someone has knocked out the back windshield.

At the edge of the woods I see the deer again. It's just standing there like it knows stuff.

Hey, I say to it. Wait.

The air is cold and sharp.

I put my hand in the pockets of my Koren Motors windbreaker. I almost scrape my knuckles on my gun.

As I walk toward the deer it starts to snow.

The flakes are so big they look fake.

A hundred million snowflakes against the black sky.

I drag my left hand across the car. FUCK YOU, it says on the door. The metal is much colder than the air and I have to make a fist.

As I pass the dead Ford Taurus I take out my gun and drop it in the front seat.

Just before I reach the deer it turns and heads into the woods.

I glance back one last time.

From the trees our house is so small it looks like you could hardly breathe in it.

A light goes on in the kitchen window.

I turn and walk into the woods.